Singing Down

THE

Preacher

Darlene Nixon

Singing Down The Preacher
Cover and Interior Page design by True Potential, Inc.
ISBN: 9781953247452 (paperback)
ISBN: 9781953247469 (ebook)
Library of Congress Control Number:

True Potential, Inc
PO Box 904, Travelers Rest, SC 29690
www.truepotentialmedia.com
Printed in the United States of America.

Cover Photo: The author's family homestead in Kentucky.

Singing Down

THE

Preacher

Foreword

Any time we learn about others, we discover something about ourselves in the process. Writing Singing Down the Preacher, I discovered my family's ancestry as Melungeons from the mountainous region of Eastern Kentucky. Melungeons are reportedly a race of people who developed in early America from the mixing of Turkish, Portuguese, Spanish, Scottish, African, and British settlers with native Cherokee Indians. The result was a beautiful people; strong, skillful, devoted, yet timid and secretive from generations of persecution.

Singing down the preacher is an old religious practice of my people where the congregation took control of the service by singing long and loud enough to let the preacher know it was time to conclude. I have come to view it as a metaphor for moments in life when we can ask God to help us take hold of situations by praying long and loud enough.

I also discovered that family doesn't necessarily mean by blood, and neighbor isn't always the one next door. This story, a fictionalized version, depicts the trials of a Melungeon family that emerged from a secluded, rustic lifestyle in the 1950s. Their struggles to survive as a family among neighbors of an unfamiliar, modern society bring to light how cruelty emerges from ignorance.

One member of the family is tested beyond comprehension. Having a learning disability makes him an easy target for those who are unaccepting of differences and wield hardened hearts. His simplistic way of thinking lands him in unsavory and even dangerous situations. Yet, it is through his simplicity that he is able to brave his fears, search for his answers, pray long and loud and in the end, receive the message that unites them all once more.

It is my hope for people to one day fully understand that we are all created in God's image and stop allowing our human differences to be a wedge that divides us. No matter how we are born, where we are born, or to whom we are born, we are each a magnificent creation. Once we can see each other in that light, then we can begin to discover how our uniqueness brings beauty to the world. And then we can discover that we are all neighbors, part of God's family. Maybe then the "Golden Rule" - Do unto others as you would have others do unto you – would be the rule rather than the exception.

I dedicate this book to my mom, Allene Watts Miller, for her shared stories that inspired my work, her persistence for discovery that gave the stories credence, and for her belief in me that kept me motivated.

Also to my husband, Hubert Nixon, whose devotion is boundless; my beautiful daughters, Jacqueline and Brooke, and all my family and friends.

Shucky Beans and Sticky Gingerbread

Residents of Lost Creek in Hazard County, Kentucky, developed the unique vegetable dish of shucky beans as a convenient staple to enjoy throughout the year. Their method of preserving green beans was much less labor-intensive than canning them in jars. Storage also proved to be a benefit, as the shriveled, dried beans took up less space.

Grown from heirloom seed, green beans were raised in every family garden. The plants would grow upward and twine around carefully placed tree limbs for easier picking. Full pods were then picked, strings carefully removed, and broken into pieces. Those lucky enough to have mesh window screen would scatter green bean pieces over the screens and allow them to dry in the sun. Others would lay their harvest on a metal rooftop for drying. Once dried, preserved beans could be stored in bags or other containers, easily keeping throughout the long winters.

The most common process, though, was to take the whole bean, remove the strings end to end, then lace a needle and thread zigzag style through the length of the bean. Strung-up pods were then suspended from the ceiling behind the kitchen woodstove, where they would dry naturally. This method provided accessible storage of their favorite vegetable.

Cooking shucky beans began with heating a generous portion of fatback in a pot for seasoning. Then they added the beans and just enough water for simmering until the "shucks" plumped up juicy and tender.

Sweets were a rarity for the mountain people. Most often, a baked sweet potato had to suffice. But on certain occasions, Mommy would bake up gingerbread cakes then roll them in a mixture of molasses, sugar, and water. The mixture formed a sweet, runny glaze that soaked deep into the cakes, melding with the pungent flavor of gingerbread for an irresistible treat.

Molasses was gleaned by community efforts then divided among families at the seasonal "stir-off." One family would raise a field of sugar cane. Yet, all families of the area would come together to reap the cane stalks, which were then placed in a horse-drawn mill to extract the juice.

At the "stir-off," juice was boiled down in a huge trough-shaped pot into a syrup. Boiling created a candy-like foam that had to be stirred and removed. Children eagerly awaited their turn to spoon off a portion of the sweet stuff—each one savoring a mouthful, as they would not taste this delicacy again for a year.

The remaining molasses was then poured into jars for all to take home. It became the main ingredient in Mommy's perfectly sticky gingerbread coating.

*****

Singing Down the Preacher

"The brimstone is ten times hotter than anything you could imagine suffering here on earth!" shouted the preacher from a make-shift stone pulpit. His frightening descriptions of hell rang in the ears and clung to the hearts of his tiny mountainside congregation.

Five-year-old Allie Watts squirmed on the blanket where she sat with her parents and nine-year-old brother, Hogan. But she struggled to keep from fidgeting too much because a switchin' from Daddy for misbehaving at church meetings could be harsh.

She pulled her wrap around her shoulders to keep out the brisk, mid-fall breeze and scratched at the braids in her hair. Mommy seemed to be ailing this morning, and her plaiting came out tighter than usual. On top of that, she hated stockings and those silly pantalettes. Why couldn't she just wear britches instead?

Glancing over at brother, she watched his face for a while. He was staring so hard at that city preacher in his fancy suit and bow tie. She only counted one blink the whole time. Then she turned to examine Mommy's belly and wondered why she was getting so fat.

"How much longer?" she whined to herself and thinking how hungry she was.

Church meetings came only once a month. Generally, three pastors from far-off towns would take turns delivering messages of Christianity. As if bound to make up for lost time, each surmounted a sermon more booming than the one before until their audience of wayward souls called a graceful end to the ravings of impending damnation.

Just then, it happened. Mr. Smith, who lived on the other side of the ridge, stood and began a slow rendition of "Amazing Grace." His family immediately rose to their feet and joined him as the last preacher continued his regaling.

One by one, members of the congregation added their voices to the cause. Little Allie happily did her part in singing down the preacher. She took hold of Hogan's hand and pushed the tune out through her throat. No matter that she didn't know all the words.

The mountainside seemed to rock and the heavens to open, receiving the thunderous waves of the familiar chorus.

"Whosoever believeth in him shall **not** die!" the preacher screamed, his hair wild from ranting and his bow tie now hanging sloppily from his lapel, "But shall have everlasting life."

His final words fell heavily as he stumbled weakly down from the rock. With that, the singing was abruptly replaced with a reverent hush that covered the meadowland. The sun began to dip toward the western sky, casting shadows where they all stood. Once again, there was peace among them.

*****

On a cold November morning in 1945, it was time. Mommy called out to Daddy, and he quickly set things in motion. Scooting Allie and John Hogan out the door, he barked at them to sound the huge cast-iron bell, which rested on a wooden pole in the yard.

Bewildered and frightened, the young brother and sister did as they were told without question. They knew tolling the bell would bring Grandma Annie. They just did not know what was so wrong with Mommy.

Grandma Annie took care of the sick in that Eastern Kentucky holler. Fevers, the gout, sometimes, even snake bites and "neumonee" (pneumonia) – this mountain medicine woman had great success healing ailments with concoctions of plants and herbs that were handed down for generations. She was also the local midwife, bringing into the world more than one member of nearly every family in Lost Creek.

After a time, the children spied their grandmother emerging from the end of the trail, which connected house to house and house to creek. She wore a simple, dark, navy blue dress with long sleeves and a high collar. The bodice was snug at the waist, but the skirt portion billowed out slightly from heavy petticoats. A full apron covered her entire front.

Brown leather lace-up boots peeked out from underneath her dress, occasionally slinging a rock with each step along the way. On top of her head sat a wide-brimmed straw hat.

As Grandma's petite stature – barely five feet, two inches – became more vivid, the children felt a great sense of relief. The sight of her familiar features, the sway of her gait, the tilt of her head, and the way she swung her black, leather medicine bag in perfect rhythm put the two at ease. She would make Mommy better. They knew she would.

"My, my." Grandma said upon reaching the edge of the yard where Allie and Hogan stood waiting, tufts, of course, gray hair escaping from her everyday bun hairdo and wafting playfully about her kindly, wrinkled face.

Annie grinned at the innocence of her grandchildren. "Now, don't y'all be frettin'. Your mommy's gonna be fine," she assured them, walking faster the closer she came to the house.

Reaching the bottom of the porch steps, Allie and Hogan stood frozen. And their grandma turned to them once more. "Go on some'ers and play. We'll talk directly." With that, she disappeared into the house, letting one of Mommy's screams out into the air.

Allie was so scared. Mommy was hurting, and she did not know why or what to do. She turned to Hogan, only to find him actually trembling. His wide, still eyes told her that he was even more scared than she. As usual, she felt beholden to take care of her older brother.

"C'mon, Hogan," she told him, taking hold of his big hand and leading him toward the nearby forest edge. "We can get some wood."

By and by, Grandma Annie appeared back out on the porch. She wiped her brow with a rag from the pocket of her apron. Cradling her tired back in the crook of a primitive, birch rocking chair, she reached into her apron again to retrieve her baccy pouch.

In ritualistic form, rough, shaky hands laid a thick line of tobacco across a torn square of brown, paper bag then carefully rolled it up and raised the homemade cigarette to craving lips.

Allie and Hogan soon caught a whiff of the familiar smoke. Dropping their armfuls of firewood, they shot out across the yard toward the aroma, sending a flock of hens squawking and flapping to get out of their path.

The noise of their stampede up the porch steps caused Grandma to laugh out loud. "Whoa up there, young'uns," she said, animating her words with a pumping motion of her arms.

Coming to an abrupt halt in front of where Grandma sat, rocking and puffing, Allie struggled to ask what preyed on her mind. "M-Mommy?" she stuttered, unsure of how to phrase the question. Hogan hung a few steps behind. Somehow, he felt safer that way.

Ominous creaking and moaning expelled from the chair runners as they rocked over pine planks. The suspense was great as Grandma leaned over to snuff out the last of her cigarette. Then, with a final exhale of billowing smoke, she gave the news they could never have imagined.

"Young'uns," their grandmother announced. "A miracle has happened."

Allie sat down Indian-style at the foot of the rocker while Hogan followed suit. Grandma held their full attention, for she had everything they needed at that moment.

"You have a new baby sister."

The world stood still for what seemed an eternity; no chattering from birds and crickets, no croaking bullfrogs or singing whippoorwills. None of the usual late afternoon mountain sounds penetrated Allie and Hogan's bewilderment. Every one of their five senses concentrated solely on the incredible announcement.

Two gaping mouths unconsciously formed the word, "How?" Grandma could see that further explanation was necessary.

"Listen here, both of you. I said it's a miracle. And I mean a true miracle from Almighty God hisself!" she insisted. "Whilst I was tendin' to your mommy, I sent your daddy to hunt some healin' roots."

At this point, each word was the most anticipated on earth. Ever the great storyteller, Grandma's eyes expressed the same wonder felt by her audience, and her voice turned to a heavenly whisper.

"And there, in a holler log, he found her – your brand new baby sister."

It was all so mind-boggling. Thus far in their young lives, they had come to accept that baby chicks hatch from eggs and seeds grow into plants. As far as baby calves and pigs were concerned, they simply seemed to appear. But never, ever had they even thought about where people babies come from, and this sudden bit of information left them completely stunned.

Yet, the hollow log story would stand, for now. The mountain people of Lost Creek were adamant about keeping their children safe from the harsh reality of such things. The thought of explaining sexuality and childbearing matters was too embarrassing – perhaps too shameful – to deal with. No matter the reason, keeping secrets for the good of all somewhere along the line became their mantra. They protected it at all costs. And so, the facts of life were left for discovery.

"Now then," Grandma began again, snapping her grandchildren out of their daze. "We've loads of work ahead. Babies take lots of attention. And your mommy's still weak from the sickness. She must stay in bed for nine days."

Feeling a sudden burst of excitement, she sputtered on. "Me an' Poppy will stay on til she's back on her feet. Oh, Lord-a-mercy, a baby is one more blessed event."

Allie wriggled with joy. She loved her grandfather, Poppy. He was so wonderfully kind and generous. Yet, Hogan remained perplexed until finally, he burst out.

"What... what's she named?" he stammered shyly.

Grandma practically squealed with delighted laughter. "I almost forgot." She grabbed up Hogan in a tight hug then turned her affection on Allie. "Let's go see her... our li'l Pearlie Sue."

*****

As the Watts children grew, they, like those before, molded into their surroundings. It never dawned on them that they were so much behind the times, so much different from the world that lay beyond their mountain boundaries.

Instead of learning how to cross a street, they were taught to follow creek banks and to count ridges for direction. While other kids were expected to use vacuum cleaners, electric washing machines, and to take neatly tied bags of trash to the curb, John Hogan, Allie, and Pearlie Sue beat rugs, scrubbed laundry with handmade lye soap, and slopped the hogs.

There were no such things as making a weekly trip to the grocery store or shopping for brand new clothes or household needs. Whatever could be grown from the land or made by hand was what they had. Occasionally, a few items could be purchased or traded from the mission house, a second-hand store operated by kindly city-Christians who wanted these mountain heathens to have a taste of civilization.

Offering used clothing, cooking utensils, blankets, and sometimes books or toys, the Riverside Mission School managed to meld into part of the culture. Because they traded for desired articles with either money or canned goods, it was not considered charity. And they all knew that charity was one of the top causes of shame.

14

A pair of half-worn boots for Hogan made him happy. With them, he could chop wood and mend cattle fences in comfort. These were his chores, and he took great pride in performing them well. Jobs that allowed him to use his full strength without requiring much thinking made him feel better about himself.

Books with only a few crumpled pages generally went to Allie. She loved to use her reading skills, always imagining that she was right there in the far-off places described. Allie was also tough and tomboyish. It was she that Mommy and Daddy relied on to make the treacherous trip up the steep ridge each evening to herd the family cattle back home from grazing.

Pearlie Sue was considered the dainty one. Her childhood, left weakened by Scarlet Fever at five years old, the family fiercely protected her. Generally, she was encouraged to stay indoors. So she gravitated toward cooking and sewing. Pearly Sue enjoyed these tasks and became very talented with a stitch. She thrilled to receive different and colorful scraps of cloth or thread from the mission house. Sometimes she would choose a pretty dolly that could be used as a model for her talent. Yet, the youngest child also developed an opinionated nature. She could discuss politics at length with Daddy or anyone else who cared to listen. This made Daddy a little too proud at times, and Mommy told him so.

"Mark my words. You'll not be so puffed up when she can't find a husband someday on account of that tongue."

The basics, however, could not be had from the mission. Baking supplies and various other necessities came from the big store in Jackson – twenty miles up the twisting creek and three ridges over to the west.

Jackson, Kentucky, was actually a small town by comparison. To the valley people, it was the big city. Jackson boasted three schools, a large mercantile store, a post office, a church, and a gas pump for those lucky enough to own an automobile.

Once each month, Mommy and Daddy would make the daylong journey into town to stock up on supplies. Most of the way was by foot. On occasion, they would meet up with someone in a truck who would be kind enough to take them the rest of the way. Yet, with no guarantee of a ride back, purchases were made carefully – only an amount that could be carried or pulled in their wooden cart.

*****

Hogan, Allie, and Pearlie Sue felt no need to complain. Why should they? This simple way of life was all they knew. They never heard of sock-hops, pajama parties, or drive-in movies.

For Nathan and Lottie, along with the other Lost Creek Families, it was more than simple tradition that sustained this way of life. There was among them and between them a great need to fulfill the directions left by prior generations.

It was not a desire to please. It was fear that compelled them. And they clung to it with all the steadfastness of mortar between bricks.

The truth of their existence lay beneath the earth of the community graveyard. A perfectly peaceful spot, the graveyard was situated on a shady, gentle slope at the base of the last ridge, which divided their world from that of mainstream America.

Every family deemed it a sacred duty to care for these grounds. Headstones marking each precious ancestor were kept free of debris. Weekly visits consisted of fond reminiscing while busily clearing the site of fallen branches, scattered leaves, and random clumps of unwanted vegetation that threatened to invade the final resting place of their beloved.

On the surface, these rituals appear as common as any other community. Yet, nothing about this secluded group of people is as it seems.

Due east of the graveyard, the great Appalachian Mountains rise out of the earth marking the opposite boundary line of the valley inhabitants. Towering above them like a massive rock wall, the mountains stand a constant barrier, holding back what their ancestors taught them to fear most: the other side.

Seemingly impenetrable, this vast mixture of jagged rock and wilderness is where their story begins. It is where two brothers by the name of Noble ventured through with their families one late fall season in 1798.

On the Virginia side of the Appalachians, John and Simpson Noble were Melungeons – a despised race of people created through the mixture of Native American Indians with the earliest invading settlers from Turkey, Portugal, Spain, and Africa. It is believed that the Indian Tribes welcomed these strange people due to their accommodating nature and the beauty of their natural dark features; thick, jet-black hair streamed down around high cheekbones, both sadness and wonder gleamed through the deepest blue eyes imaginable and all carried by strong, firm bodies sustained through daily hard labor.

As outcasts from the land across the ocean, it only felt natural to set up villages in this new land with people who accepted them so openly. Freedom was finally theirs, if only for a short time.

The beginning of the end came with the eventual British Colonies that sprang up along the coast and spread westward. While some of the white people were drawn to the Melungeon beauty and spirit, the majority repelled them. They were deemed inferior, and association with them was frowned upon.

Still, human nature being what it is, the Melungeon race was further complicated by the genes of those Brits, Scots, Frenchmen, and other Whites who could not resist. Some of the offspring came into the world with light enough skin and features to cause much confusion among the colonists determined to segregate themselves from the "low-life, mixed-breed of people."

Unable to take Melungeons as slaves, colony leaders passed laws denoting them a "free race of color." Such a maneuver denied their unorthodox neighbors the right to vote or to even live among the colonists, which included attending schools and churches. However misguided, it seemed to give the white colonists power over their fears.

Pushed further and further into the mountains, the forlorn people took into their souls deep shame for not being good enough. And their seclusion brought on great hardships for day-to-day survival. Yet, survive they did. Drawing from lessons taught by their native Indian friends, some developed fine skills of gardening and hunting. Others discovered talents in stone and woodworking.

They planted and hammered out a meager existence, all the while dreaming and scheming ways to fit in with those "lucky" people down below. Eventually, some of the "white" looking Melungeons were able to masquerade their way into the colonial world. Casting off their Melungeon heritage, they married partners who were willing to risk being outcasts themselves.

This bit of success by some gave hope to others. Being Melungeon meant nothing but misery. There could never be any celebrating of their beginnings or rejoicing for the sacrifices made by those who first set foot on the land now called America. So, decisions were made that by hiding their true identity, they might escape the current ill-fated situation. In order to move forward, they would have to leave a part of them behind.

Looking straight up to the top of the mighty Appalachians, John and Simpson Noble were among those who envisioned a better life for their families on the other side. They could shed these god-forsaken Melungeon shackles and start anew. Why couldn't there be people over there just as welcoming as their Indian friends had been?

*****

John awoke early that morning. It was late October. A frosty fog hung heavy across the mountainside. He stepped purposefully over to the barnyard where the family wagons were loaded and ready to move.

One last check of supplies: cans of coffee, bags of green beans dried over the past summer, called shucky beans, and sacks of flour, cornmeal, and sugar. All were heaped atop trunks, which contained blankets and clothing. Just within reach lay two muskets and plenty of gunpowder.

Tied behind, the family milk cow stood nonchalantly chewing her cud. John argued against bringing her. He didn't think she could make the trip. But Sally was adamant about having fresh milk for as long as possible. In the end, he agreed, believing that if the animal gave out, there would at least be an extra source of meat.

The countryside seemed paralyzed, not a sound to be heard. Movement came only from the gentle lifting of the fog, giving way to brilliant red streaks that billowed across the sky. As the sun slowly pushed upward, John looked down toward the colony below. It all seemed so final.

Turning away from the horizon, he noticed his brother, Simpson, coming around the bend. The younger Noble was dressed fully in buckskin. Heavy boots clanked on his feet with every step as he expertly balanced a laden backpack between his broad shoulders.

The two met up at the wagon, each giving the other a nod of readiness, knowing, and yet, not knowing what lay ahead.

"We should be heading out soon," Simpson advised. "Day's a waistin'."

"I'll get the wife then," John replied, already walking toward their tiny cabin.

It had become known to them only a few weeks before that his wife, Sally, was pregnant. The young, outcast couple earnestly dreamed of bringing their child into a kinder world. Preparations for this venture began almost immediately.

Sally, the granddaughter of a full Cherokee Indian, was tall and slender with fiery blue eyes. She was full of spirit, which only added to her immense beauty. As a young girl, Sally drew much attention from the colonist boys. During visits for supplies, it was obvious to her parents that she should one day attract a colonist husband, giving her a chance at freedom from the bondage of their race. How distressed they were when, head-strong, she announced affections for John Noble, the handsome son of a neighboring Melungeon family.

Refusing to believe she was less of a person, Sally carried herself in a prideful manner, often to the chagrin of her new husband. Many times she received scoldings for admiring her thick, lush hair during brushings or for displaying too much happiness while trying on a newly sewn dress.

"You will surely get back double in sadness for all this boasting!" he warned her on several occasions. "It says so in the Good Book."

Wanting so much to please her husband, she worked hard at containing these feelings. However, her high-strung nature would reach far into generations ahead, despite the strictest of parental teachings.

Brother Simpson had not yet chosen a wife. He had been much too occupied with perfecting his hunting and woodworking skills. By peddling some of his wooden masterpieces to the villagers, he was able to accumulate a small bit of wealth. Most of the village people were unaware that their beautiful pieces of furniture and sturdy wagons and plows were Melungeon-made. The crafty Noble brother slipped down the mountain at night to meet the shop owner, who also profited handsomely from the skills of his secret supplier.

Although Simpson longed to have his name carved prominently on the back of his work, he played the necessary game and was honored to be able to aid his brother and sister-in-law on this journey. His money and talent would certainly be useful.

Sunrise found the trio trudging upward along a rocky pathway, their worldly possessions packed up tight with their hopes and dreams.

As they progressed higher into the mountains than they had ever been, the pathway closed into a treacherous trail. Thin, cold air pressed against their lungs. Two weeks into the trip, John's prediction came true. Their cow could no longer continue. Without ample grass for grazing, she no longer produced milk. There was no grain to spare for her sustenance, and the hills were now too steep to keep pulling her along. Late one evening, John carried his musket and led her just out of eyesight. With no other choice, he ended her journey at the edge of a rocky cliff.

Two more weeks of this pace tested each of their wills further than imaginable. Bitter cold came in at the end of November. They trudged daily through fresh snows and huddled together under the wagon at night. Winds howled over them angrily as they prayed to God for deliverance. They prayed constantly; prayed for sure feet over cliffs and boulders; prayed for strength inside and out. But mostly, they prayed for this test of endurance to bring the peace they so desired.

At this height, wildlife became more scarce. Rations ran low. Finding a stream where the ice was breakable enough to retrieve water was a constant worry. In the past few days, their journey had taken a slow descent. Surely they were on the other side now. They had to be more than halfway. Doubts cluttered their minds; each day which proved even crueler than the last. Would they succumb to this hellish environment just as the cow had?

Still, each evening, John offered up a sort of sermon. He pulled out the tattered Bible given him by his mother. Although he couldn't read the words, he held the book open and repeated verses he memorized as a child. He spoke every word he could think of to spur on encouragement and hope. His voice grew louder and louder while pages rattled and God's words swelled through the atmosphere.

"Whosoever believeth in me shall not die but have everlasting life!"

Simpson and Sally participated fully in their pretend church service. Just as they had done back home, they offered "Amens!" and "Hallelujahs!" throughout. Until, having enough, the tiny congregation of two lifted up their voices in song, finally overpowering the designated preacher in a harmonious signal to close the service.

One particularly bright morning, John rose earlier than the rest of his family. A feeling had come over him to walk straight westward. Eventually, he reached a patch of poplar and birch trees that beckoned him closer. As if in a trance, he followed a deer trail through it. The ground seemed much more level. Just ahead, boulders rounded out of the earth like pillars to the gates of heaven.

In an elated state, John rushed toward the rocks and found himself peering over to the most beautiful creek bottom, wooded on one side, clear on the other. He lifted red, chapped hands up to his face and allowed rears to run down them as he surveyed the perfect valley below.

Visions of a thriving garden stood next to a cabin with gentle puffs of smoke emitting from the fireplace. He could swear he actually smelled the aroma of a huge pot of shucky beans simmering. Turning to his left, the Melungeon pioneer noticed a row of hollowed-out boulders. He knew instantly that these caves would provide his family a perfect temporary shelter. They could live in the rock houses, as they called them, while they worked at developing their brand new settlement.

"Once I was lost, but now I'm found," John muttered triumphantly to himself. He believed with all his heart that God had led them to this "creek for the lost," and he would spend his life working to build a prosperous community that would keep his people safe from the evils endured on the other side of the world.

Indeed, the Nobles set up a fine homestead on the Kentucky side of the Appalachians. Between John's green thumb and Simpson's marksmanship, hunger was the least of their worries. And just when they began to grow lonely for other human companionship, the discovery of a nearby Cherokee Indian Tribe filled the void with a shared peace between kindred spirits.

Through the weeks and months to come, the clans melded together as if by design, sharing skills and knowledge that ensured a greater survival and a stronger bond. Before long, other Melungeons made their way over the mountains, bringing with them tales of great persecution from which they fled and great sadness over lost loved ones along the way. Some were even mixed colonists and Melungeon families, escaping even more cruel torment at being "despicable creatures."

As the community grew, setting down rules became a necessity. With his strength of character and deep belief in fairness, John accepted the task as leader. Sally was never so proud of her husband as when she heard him speak in front of the entire community. She rocked their baby son and smiled up at him as he told them all how they must start being plain ordinary people and not Melungeon.

"It's the only way," he announced. "We must never speak of being Melungeon again. For the sake of our children, we must never tell them of our true heritage. When the white people come, and they will come, we must say only that we are French and Indian and nothing more."

John continued to tell the group that the Indian Chief told him of fur traders crossing through the area. He fervently believed it was only a matter of time before other settlements, white settlements, sprang up on this side of the mountains.

While his intentions were purely honorable, John could never have known the far-reaching impact of his speech. The people of Lost Creek took this deceit of their identity fully to heart, blurring it into distrust. Although, as generations came and went, secrets of a Melungeon past did slip out from a few elders who could not resist telling heroic stories of their escape across the mountains. Added to these tales were strict instructions not to reveal them to outsiders. However innocent, this practice of silence bred a feeling that isolation equaled safety. Discovery meant a risk of more persecution.

Ironically, many of the white people who eventually did come further west to conquer new territory also brought with them knowledge of lowly Melungeons. As white towns developed high above Lost Creek, descendants of America's first settlers sank deeper into seclusion and further out of history's pages.

Even though the name of their true race all but vanished, the same old feelings of prejudice, fear, and distrust remained strong. "Free Race of Color" became the description of choice by white town governments, which kept all Noble descendants from having the freedom they still sought to find.

Scattered through the generations, however, were born those who carried Sally's strong-spirited nature. Like her, they refused to accept any talk about not belonging or not being good enough. Great pride manifested itself in bucking the system, in walking through town with a head held high, in sneaking into classrooms to learn how to read, in generally pushing their way into every area deemed out-of-bounds.

For some, this spirit led to actions outside of respectability and even outside the law. During the Prohibition Era, resources for making an honest living were extremely limited. Bootlegging whiskey proved too profitable to pass up. Possessing an unlimited supply of shine led to overconsumption, which brought about such undesirable attributes as greed and a mean, uncaring nature. Soon, the mysterious Melungeons - bootleggers or not – were given the title of sly, dangerous creek dwellers.

Desperate to maintain order, the elders relied on ancient superstitions to bring about obedience. They wholeheartedly believed every word. But the idea was meant to keep the mind sharp and to always be on the lookout for trouble.

The most obscure superstition stated, "Never turn around in the middle of a trip to get a forgotten item, lest you befall a terrible fate." To avoid such great devastation, you must first mark an X in the path with your foot then spit in the mark before heading back.

"Burning corn cobs from your garden will cause your next crop to burst into flames," warned another rule of the hollow. Yet, the most familiar and most feared saying denounced any form of a happy-go-lucky attitude. "Do not show too much happiness or double the sadness will follow."

*****

By the 1950s, only one modern-day convenience infiltrated the Watts Family's home – the radio. Over the years, it announced news of World War II, the great depression, and the political goings-on of several presidential elections.

Through the airwaves, Daddy became highly educated in these matters. He could discuss them at great length with anyone who cared to listen. He also became a staunch democrat, campaigning in his own way for the one who gained his complete admiration, President Franklin D. Roosevelt. Daddy trusted FDR's every word and was convinced that eventually, the "New Deal Program" developed by "The only Commander-In-Chief" as far as he was concerned would save them.

The children were not allowed to listen to such grown-up topics. But they didn't mind. Come Saturday night, the Grand Ole Opry filled their house and hearts with music and laughter. Each week, a mystified group sat around the magical battery-operated box in awe of the melodious sounds it released into the room.

Mommy's favorite song was "Rocky Top." She sang along in perfect harmony to the delight of her three children, who attempted to dance a jig in time with banjo pickings.

Daddy mostly scoffed at the so-called entertainment. His interest was held by the daily struggle of supporting his family. Mommy watched in sadness to see her kind, gentle-hearted husband grow more solemn and withdrawn at the slipping of each opportunity.

He wanted to serve his country during the war. But a medical examination by the Army detected back problems and a heart murmur. Daddy knew his back hurt all the time. He also knew he had to keep on working. So he didn't understand why they wouldn't take him. He also soon found out there was no arguing with government officials.

Carpentry was Nathan Watts' true gift. A number of the cozy and solid cabins that lined their hillside resulted from his talent. He also made beautiful pieces of wood furniture, much like his ancestor, Simpson Noble. But friends and neighbors could scarcely afford his services, so he made money by working in nearby coal mines.

After a few years of breathing coal dust daily took its toll on Daddy's lungs. Several nights spent wheezing and coughing up blood forced the couple to make a drastic decision. A cousin of Nathan's had been making decent wages picking green beans for a canning factory up north in Indiana. There was work in the north, but Nathan would have to be gone most of the summer. At least he would be outdoors, breathing fresh air, and he could send money home like he wanted to if he had joined the Army. It seemed like the only way.

Summer lasted forever while Daddy was away. Mommy's heart ached to be separated from her husband. Still, she carried on, tending a meticulous garden, keeping a spotless home, and teaching her children all they needed to know about maintaining a home place in the hills. She took them on evening walks in the woods, pointing out by name every plant and tree in their path, along with each specific use or danger.

Allie paid particular attention to these lessons. She loved nature, reveling in the presence of all living things. For her, there was no greater joy than to know she possessed the ability to seek out ginseng roots and other special leaves for Grandma Annie's medicines. For someone who could become easily agitated at people, Allie held all the patience in the world with all God's other creatures.

Once, during mid-summer, Allie set her mind on catching a live hummingbird. "Why not?" she wondered, thinking about all the other animals she had outsmarted and captured in the past – runaway banty hens, crickets, fish, even a sparrow or two. A hummingbird, she decided, would be a great catch.

Summing up her challenge at hand, the young mountain girl watched for hours as the tiny creature hovered around a butterfly bush at the corner of their house. Its delicate wings beat feverishly while darting in and out of blooms looking for nectar. Allie determined that she could sit completely still for as long as it took until her target believed she was actually part of the flowering plant.

Day after day, she held her position, watching and waiting. Just as she expected, the dainty little bird became comfortable enough with her presence to inch closer toward the dark, summer skin of Allie's hand. Afraid to breathe, she watched her humming friend ease just within reach. Her heart pounded as wildly as the bird's wings in anticipation of the impending attempt. Then, in one lightning-fast swooping motion, Allie's hand grabbed the bird and pulled it to her side. She ran to the house to show Mommy her triumph, who could hardly believe she saw a live humming-bird struggling and squawking in her eldest daughter's hands.

All the children missed Daddy during these summers. But Hogan seemed especially lost. After all, it was Daddy who taught him to cut wood and build fences. And it was Daddy who made him feel safe when the rest of the world appeared so intimidating.

At age 17, Hogan had grown into a tall, handsome man with a shapely chest and full, round muscles. Inside, however, a child still controlled his thoughts and actions. Other young men of his age had already left the schoolyard in search of work and wives. A lucky few found a way to attend the college up in Jackson. But timid and awkward, Hogan could not think of himself being anywhere except on their familiar homestead.

Although he was a great help to Mommy, she worried incessantly about her son's condition. She knew he was not what others considered normal. He struggled with school lessons well beneath his age level. Oftentimes, very simple instructions seemed just beyond his grasp. A meek and gentle creature, Hogan bore the brunt of many a cruel joke.

Her son's obvious shortcomings tugged at Mommy daily, thinking how she might have prevented his predicament. She remembered back to when she was pregnant, living with Nathan's parents. Her mother-in-law, Naomi, was a heartless woman who never wanted them to marry.

Young Lottie suffered miserably under Naomi's cruel mental and physical retaliation. But she took all the harsh words. "I told Nathan you weren't fittin'. Can't you do no better than that? I don't know why Nathan had to ruin himself with the likes of you." Throughout her delicate condition, she managed the tough chores required and the countless nights of hunger pains when Naomi only allowed very small portions at supper. Not wanting to cause trouble between her husband and his family, she endured it all.

Shortly after Hogan arrived, the new family moved into a cabin that Nathan built. Lottie breathed a sigh of relief. Her baby appeared fine, and now they were able to live peacefully on their own. Yet tragedy struck just two years later. Whooping cough swept through the valley like a wildfire, claiming the lives of a dozen babies and children.

Annie could scarcely make it to one house before another bell began ringing. Day after day, she consoled heartbroken mothers whose cries pierced the cold January air.

When Hogan began the first signs of the dreaded childhood sickness, Lottie grabbed up her little boy and prayed hard. She took the rubbing compress Annie made for them just in case and applied it to Hogan's wheezing chest. She rocked and prayed for hours as the hacking grew deeper and more frequent.

In between coughs, Hogan cried, which brought on more coughing and praying. The cycle continued to escalate until Lottie felt powerless. Then came the moment when all noise ceased. Looking down at her baby, Lottie noticed that he hadn't just fallen asleep. He wasn't breathing at all. Gripped in horror, she watched his arms flailing in an attempt to gasp for air.

"No!" she screamed, jumping up from the rocker and racing to the kettle for another hot compress. She massaged her son's chest and begged God to let him live. A few minutes seemed like hours, but she refused to give up. In desperation and anger, she shook Hogan, ordering him to breathe. Harder and harder, she shook until, as if by miracle, the air was forced back into his lungs. A sputtering cry turned gradually louder and louder, along with Lottie's thankful sobbing. It was the sweetest sound she had ever heard.

Now, watching her grown son, Mommy could not help but wonder if any of these things played a part in his being so different. Her mind trembled with thoughts of guilt and regret. If only she had stood up to Naomi, or if she had protected him better.

*****

Pearlie Sue grew into a tall, petite young woman. Even though she dreamed of doing something incredible with her life, she never really expected to be anything other than a homemaker like all the other women of their family. It wasn't that she had anything in particular against hard work or the outdoors. In fact, she was the one who helped Mommy with the heavy cleaning chores while Hogan and Allie seemed to be always rambling around in the woods. Still, she simply preferred to busy herself with skills of embroidery, quilting, and baking. While she did accompany her family on evening walks, she would rarely be found outside during the heat of the day. Pearlie Sue took to heart Grandma Annie's warning that too much sun would make her "brown as a biscuit."

While she didn't really understand her people's aversion to a dark tan, she did so want to please and took every precaution to guard her complexion. Her thick, long hair waved gracefully to a delicate curling at the ends and was much easier to brush than Allie's.

With her slender build and generally sweet disposition, Mommy and Daddy found it easy to believe their youngest daughter was fragile. There were never any intentions of favoritism. Mommy and Daddy loved all their children the same. They simply felt there would be hardships in store for Pearlie Sue that they would not be able to prevent. So, making her life as pleasant as possible for as long as possible seemed appropriate.

Sometimes Pearlie Sue would protest their over-protectiveness by quoting a political statement she heard from Daddy or something more physical such as lagging behind on a walk to brave a rattlesnake path at dusk.

At any rate, the brother and sisters were no longer little children, and their futures loomed precariously ahead.

*****

One particular summer's end brought more than a change of season. As normal, Lottie was elated to see her husband emerging up the path from the creek. This time, however, her glad expression quickly turned to a face filled with concern as she noticed him limping and grimacing with pain.

After supper that evening, he explained how he would no longer be able to make the trip up north.

"I saw a doctor in Austin. He says my back won't take all the stooping over anymore, and if I keep on, I might not be able to walk at all."

"But what will we do, Nathan?" Lottie asked him, her eyes sinking in fear.

"This doctor gave me a paper. He called them orders."

Nathan continued describing the situation as though it were the best thing in the world. Taking the paper out of his sweaty pocket, he showed it to Lottie while bracing up his best worry-free smile.

"It says here that I can't work and I can get the welfare money from the government, just like President Roosevelt said. We'll have fifty dollars come to the post office each month. That should be plenty to get us by."

Lottie could hardly believe it. She wiped a tear of relief with the hem of her apron then clasped her hands joyfully to her heart.

"You mean you don't ever have to leave us again? We can all be together, and we don't have to worry about money?" she asked hesitantly.

"That's what I mean," he assured her, fiercely trying not to be too happy. The last thing he wanted was for great sadness to find them tomorrow.

****

Allie was mad, fightin' mad. Her hot-tempered nature flared like a fire out of control. Schoolbooks held by a strap bounced hard across her back with every determined step. But she could hardly feel a thing. Rocks along the pathway home felt no mercy from swift kicks as they hurled through the air and landed with a great kerplunk into the creek.

She did not notice that Hogan and Pearlie Sue trailed her from a safe distance, fearful of what her fury might bring. As she came in sight of their house, it never occurred to her that Mommy was not outside waiting for them with her usual smile and open arms.

The anger Allie felt overshadowed all her senses. She couldn't remember a time when she had been this mad. She stood up to the kids at school plenty of times on Hogan's behalf. This was different, worse, even worse than the day she ran home from school, terrified that she was dying. Mommy had a time calming down her hysterical teenager long enough to assure her that the blood was just a natural part of life for a woman.

"It's a curse that God put on us," Mommy told her, reminding her of the Bible story when Eve disobeyed God by eating the apple in the Garden of Eden. "All we can do is bear it," she concluded.

Allie didn't want to bear it. For weeks she was mad at Eve and at God. Lately, it seemed as if she were mad at the whole world. Confusing thoughts welled up in her mind, though she dared not speak of them. Sometimes she wanted to be held like a baby; sometimes, to be left completely alone. Other times, she wanted to run far away and scream aloud until her body stretched enough to hold all of her feelings.

Now she thought she would actually explode. Her anger swelled as surely as the nose on Billy Jackson's face had done in the schoolyard.

Inside the house, Allie could contain herself no longer.

"Mommy, them Jackson boys said we were liars and cheats!"

she shouted, forgetting for the moment that outbursts by children were strictly forbidden.

"You best mind your manners, young lady," Daddy warned sternly from his chair.

"Yes'ir" she muttered, choking back the flood of emotions. She still had not noticed the gloomy air circulating in the room.

Mommy caressed Allie's hand and led her over to sit at the table.

"What's a matter, child? Why did they say those things?"

Allie couldn't get the words out fast enough.

"They say we took the government money for no good reason," she sputtered through tears. "They told everybody that you and Daddy lied to them welfare people. I told 'em it weren't true. Then Billy said his daddy called us same as crooks and we would all burn in hell!"

Hogan and Pearlie Sue slipped in during their sister's tirade. Pearlie Sue went straight over to Allie in alliance. Hogan stayed close to the door; his head hung low in shame.

After getting a nod from Daddy, Mommy gathered them all around the table. Three sets of wide eyes peered at her for answers. Spurts of Allie's sobs broke the initial silence. The aroma of sweet potatoes baking and a pot of shucky beans on the stove let them know they were still breathing. They all wished Poppie and Grandma Annie were there.

"There's no reason to be 'shamed," Mommy announced first off. "We ain't done a thing wrong."

True enough, the families of Lost Creek became jealous of Nathan and Lottie getting "free money" when their men had to work in the coal mines or travel away to earn a living. Allowing jealousy to cloud the reality of their neighbors' true situation, a few of them made false reports to the welfare office of seeing Nathan working in his garden, chopping wood, and other activities a "real disabled" man could not do.

Such testimonies were meant to make right what seemed unfair. Unfortunately, nothing in the system allowed for a hearing of both sides. Nathan and Lottie received word that very morning. They would no longer receive the government money, just as the Jackson's hoped. Cracks in President Roosevelt's "New Deal" failed them, leaving Nathan troubled and more withdrawn.

While their children were at school, the coupled fretted over a future, finally deciding they had no other choice. Hogan would have to quit school and make a living for the family. Yet, neither of them wanted to send him off to the mines. They would not put their son in that danger. The only way was to leave Lost Creek and move the family to Indiana, where Hogan could find a decent job.

"We just can't make a living here no more," Mommy said plainly. "But the Lord helps them that helps themselves. And your daddy says we can do fine in that town where he worked summers.

She paused, examining the shocked looks on her children's faces.

"We're moving to Austin, Indiana."

"All of us?" Allie asked

"Poppie and Grandma Annie too?" quizzed Pearlie Sue.

"No," Mommy answered apologetically. "Just us. Poppie and Grandma are too old to go anywhere. But don't worry. They'll get along same as always. Right now, we have to take care of each other."

Three young people struggled silently with the news. Three imaginations ran wild, frantically attempting to comprehend the incomprehensible. They would never question Mommy or Daddy. Still, the thought of leaving the only place they had ever known was more than their minds could absorb.

Hogan thought of Aunt Lilly. He pictured her face. She was so pretty, and she always smelled of the vanilla flavoring that she dabbed bed his whittling but continued to look straight down. He knew she was about to say something he didn't want to hear, and he couldn't bear to face her.

But Lilly knelt down in front of him and squeezed his hand. She wasn't good at breaking news gently, and most of the time, she didn't care. Already, she brushed off the disappointment from the rest of the family. Even the ravings of her mother, Naomi, who cursed the wickedness of the world Lilly sought, caused little emotion.

Hogan was so genuine in his simplicity. He never appeared to think badly of her, no matter what others said. She badly wanted to make him understand and not be sad. If only she knew the right words.

"You won't ever see me again." Lilly finally resigned herself to the abrupt announcement. "I'm going to California. Do you know where that is?"

Hogan shook his head but still did not look up. He focused on her hands and the red color on her fingernails. He had never seen colored fingernails before.

"California is on the other side of the world," she tried to explain. "There's a whole other ocean out there, and California is right beside it. I'm going there to find what makes me happy. Do you understand?"

Again, Hogan only shook his head.

Talking primarily to herself, Lilly continued.

"Everybody around here says they are happy to be at the bottom of this God-forsaken mountain. But just look at them. Nobody ever smiles. They're all too afraid to be happy. Well, not me. I look at the pictures in the catalogs and see such pretty people with smiles so wide you would think they might break. I want to be where people smile like that. I don't want to end up a frowning, frightened old lady."

When she finished, Lilly looked up at her naïve, young nephew. Although she knew he didn't understand anything she said, she also knew he wouldn't judge her for saying it. She rose from her knees and softly kissed his cheek.

"Just remember always that I love you and whenever you see California on a map, think of me smiling."

Lilly walked slowly down the porch steps and onto the path. Hogan breathed in the last whiff of her perfume, pondering for several minutes how far away California must be before he picked up his whittling again. The only thing he knew for sure was that he would always remember that moment.

Having thought of it, Hogan interrupted the conversation. "How far is California from Indiana?" he asked.

"Goodness, child. Much farther than we could ever go," Mommy answered with astonishment. "What in the world made you think of California?"

"Aunt Lilly is there, isn't she? I thought we might could visit her."

"Lord-a-mercy," Mommy said with a half-grin, amazed at his strong memory. "I don't think we could make it that far away from the Smokies. But don't you worry,

none of you. We'll be just fine in Indiana because we'll be together and take care of each other."

*****

Word spread quickly throughout the hillsides of the family's intentions to leave by summer's end. Whispers of astonishment and hostile indignation breezed from neighbor to neighbor. Even the Jacksons, whose cruel lies had caused the Wattes' plight, turned their heads in disbelief.

Nathan and Lottie were at a loss to understand the contradictory actions of their people. They took away the only possibility of making a living, yet they found fault in the family leaving as a means of survival. It seemed unacceptable for any member of their community to enjoy any sort of comfortable life. Even more unacceptable was the idea of abandoning the clan.

"It just ain't right." they were told by neighbors who scoffed at their decision. "The Nobles meant for us all to stay here and protect our land. Too many of our young people have gone already. Curse be on you if the rest follow."

True enough, others had gone before, primarily sons who joined the military and found better lives. A few were sent by missionaries to attend school in larger cities. Rarely did an entire family pick up and move.

Naomi's bitterness at her only remaining son leaving flashed with cruel threats. While she disowned Lilly long before her departure, Naomi defended her eldest son, Ben, for starting a new life in Indiana. She would never forgive Nathan, however, and absolutely blamed Lottie.

"In all my born days, I never thought Nathan would desert me," she stated coldly. "Pa and I are getting on in years. Everyone else is gone. It's your duty to stay and look after us."

Grandma Annie and Poppie also felt great sadness at losing their daughter. Only the year before, they allowed Lottie's younger brother to go stay at a boarding house in Jackson so he could attend the college there. Besides, tradition dictated that women should remain close enough to tend to aging parents, and they made every opportunity to remind her of it.

Laden with guilt, they continued the daunting task of deciding what to pack and what to leave. Livestock had to be dealt with. Meat from the smokehouse and jars of vegetables from the root cellar had to be distributed among family. Still, they wondered about the ways of their people. How could it be better to drag each other down rather than rejoice in one of their own's good fortune?

Ironically, it was Nathan's brother, Ben, who encouraged them to come to Austin. He promised to get Hogan a job at the local cannery, and they could live with him and his family until they found a house of their own.

Ben had worked in the green bean fields alongside Nathan for several summers. Labor in the canning factory was considered a step up. Finally able to land a position himself, he didn't waste any time convincing one of the foremen to give his strong, young nephew a chance. While the work was indoors and standing replaced constantly stooping over rows of green bean plants, the days were still long, and the ever-flowing steam emitted from rows of six-foot-tall metal vats filled with blanched beans could be stifling.

They all felt that Hogan should have no trouble grasping such a repetitive job. He certainly did not mind hard work. He only needed clear, simple instructions and a little encouragement every once in a while. Ben respected the supervisor who agreed to hire Hogan. He assured his brother and sister-in-law that their son would be treated well.

Hogan himself did not know how to react to the situation at hand. Pangs of nervousness accompanied his thoughts as he wondered about everything. He wondered about the town called Austin and the job that Mommy and Daddy told him about. Yet, a factory that did nothing but put up green beans all day was more than he could imagine. What a huge family that must be, he thought.

Mostly though, he thought about Mommy saying he had become

a man. He had no idea what it should feel like to be a man. But he still didn't think he felt like one. Finally, he decided that it must be because he had grown as tall as Daddy and could beat any of the kids at Leatherwood School at arm wrestling.

*****

On the hottest dog day of the summer, a day when no other mountain creature dared stir, the Watts Family began their journey out of Kentucky. Having no mechanical means of transportation meant taking only a few clothes and possessions. Whatever could be toted comfortably was tucked into Army duffle bags that Daddy got from the Mission. Everything else would be fine til they could make arrangements.

Mommy walked outside first. She surveyed her garden patch one last time. It was the most beautiful garden she could remember. Varieties of lush, green bean vines twined their way up healthy stalks of yellow sweet corn. Tomato bushes hung heavy with fruit next to rows of summer squash and hills of sweet potatoes.

"Grandma Annie and Poppie will make good use of it," she thought to console herself. She would make another one just as pretty next year, in the backyard of their new home.

Soon, Daddy called to her. She swiftly plucked five juicy, ripe tomatoes for the walk. Cradling the fruit in her apron, she hurried to join the family down the pathway out of Lost Creek.

A day's walk later, they arrived at the bus station. Hot, tired and grungy with sweat, Mommy and the children huddled on a waiting bench while Daddy purchased their tickets with money made from selling their farm animals. He also bought them each a pack of crackers and a small carton of milk from the station café. He felt bad for not having more as he passed out the small snacks. But it would have to make due until they got to Ben's house the next morning.

Feeling very much like fish out of water, the children marveled at such fancy surroundings. They had been to Jackson a few times before to help bring back groceries or to get mail from the Post Office. However, the bus station represented the unknown. It was a gateway to another world, and they fretted over what might be on the other side. A voice over the loudspeaker caused them to nearly jump out of their skin. Deep and ominous, the voice delivered messages of new arrivals and departures.

Their bus would be leaving soon, according to the man's words from above. So, at Mommy's insistence, the children visited the station facilities. Anxious to see what a city outhouse looked like, the girls tugged hard at the heavy, swinging door as if something amazing would happen just by its opening.

Allie giggled aloud at her sister's reaction to the swooshing sound of the flushing commode.

"I've never heard water sound like that," Pearlie Sue admitted timidly.

"Me either," Allie agreed. "But it sure smells better than our outhouse."

The girls had a good laugh, washed their hands and faces, then met up with Hogan and their parents, who were already waiting to board.

As tired as they were and as sternly as Daddy instructed, the siblings found it difficult to stay asleep. They felt every bump. The wheels made loud whirring noises while city lights and vehicle headlights shone through the windows, keeping their attention on everything but rest.

Eventually, however, they did sleep. Just as Daddy promised, they awoke to find themselves at the Austin, Indiana Bus Station.

Eighteen-year-old Hogan, fifteen-year-old Allie, and ten-year-old Pearlie Sue stepped out into the daylight in full view of this new town. Their newly awakened eyes could not keep up with all the bustling activity. People dressed as neatly as for church meetings scurried to and fro. Motor vehicles sped up and down the street in front of them, with horns honking and lights flashing. A myriad of voices talking, laughing, and yelling cluttered the air around them as they stood awe struck.

"Why is everyone in such a hurry?" asked Allie, as she spied a short, white bus-like vehicle drive by that had a large picture of a milk jar painted on the side.

"This is just how they live," Daddy answered, still grumpy from the long ride, which aggravated his aching back. "These people are all going to where they work."

Suddenly, a familiar voice called to them, and each head turned to see Ben motioning toward his truck. Hogan and Allie grabbed the duffle bags while following their parents, who had a hold of Pearlie Sue.

The ride to Ben's house took them clear through town. How silly it seemed to stop every few feet at a street corner. Yet Allie and Pearlie Sue could think of no words as their uncle drove them past the high school. In a few short weeks, they would have to go there alone. It was a brick two-story building with concrete steps and another large building called the "Gymnasium" in the back. Allie shuddered to think of being inside there with all those different kids. She thought she would never be able to learn them all.

Around the corner of another street stood a building that seemed to stretch for miles in front of them. A metal fence enclosed the entire facility. Everyone in the truck watched for several minutes as a line of men and women descended into the main entrance. Overhead, a sign read "Morgan Cannery, Inc."

Hogan picked out the word "can" and knew immediately that this intimidating place must be where he was to start work. A shiver of nervousness rushed through his body. This was Friday. He was to go with Uncle Ben first thing Monday morning.

"Here we are," Ben announced as he steered the old pickup truck into his driveway.

Mommy could not get over how close the houses were to each other. You could actually see in the neighbor's window from your window. She closed her eyes for a moment and took a deep breath, telling herself that in time she would get used to it.

Taking hold of Pearlie Sue's hand, she helped her youngest down from the cab of the truck. The door closed behind them with a giant creak as though signaling the closing of their past behind.

Hogan and Allie climbed out from the truck bed while cautiously surveying up one side of Walnut Street then down the other. Residents passing by on the sidewalk appeared just as cautious. A friendly-looking woman pushing a baby stroller smiled briefly while keeping a steady pace. Two other ladies out for a morning walk barely glanced their way as they continued an apparently engrossing conversation. And a group of kids riding bicycles slowed down only long enough to giggle and point before racing off.

Sounds of unfamiliar human activity seemed to come from every direction. Noises of doors closing, tools clanking, motors running, children playing, and parents calling to children replaced the comforting quiet of nature.

Finally, the family made their way inside. Not much bigger than the cabin in Lost Creek, the house did at least contain three separate bedrooms – one was Uncle Ben and Aunt Jean's, Cousin Sissy shared her room with the girls, while Hogan and the boys; Leon and little Benny, took the living room for sleeping quarters to accommodate Nathan and Lottie in the last room.

Standing face to face for the first time, the cousins greeted each other warmly with a hint of wariness. Knowing they were all kin did not take away the sense of meeting strangers. Back home, children were taught early to always hold suspicion for strangers.

Allie looked around the room. Her first glance noticed walls painted white from corner to corner. "How odd," she thought.

At the back of one wall sat a long, cushioned piece of furniture, she later learned was a couch. Rocking chairs sat at each end with lamp tables in between. On the opposite wall, a small table held a fancy radio. It had two funny-looking metal sticks stretching out of the top. Allie dared not ask any questions for fear of being laughed at. Instead, she prayed hard that she might learn these modern ways before encountering all the people at school.

"Would you like to see the garden?" Jean asked Lottie, finally breaking the awkward silence. "We have some real nice Kentucky Wonders. I thought we'd pick a mess for supper."

Aunt Jean smiled, motioning for her sister-in-law to follow. Lottie obliged the request, and the two soon disappeared into the kitchen then out the back with a soothing creak of a screen door.

An Austin native, Jean differed completely from anyone the Watts children ever knew. Robust in stature, she carried herself with confidence. Her open personality shown through emerald green eyes, which mesmerized her newfound relatives, and her skin was so light they figured she must never go out in the sun. Her straight hair, as blonde as buttermilk, was cut above her shoulders, sporting a huge curl that flipped out along the end.

Pearlie Sue felt her own coarse, plaited hair. She didn't mean to, but she couldn't help envying her aunt and cousin, Sissy, just a little.

Ben met and married Jean on his first summer working in the bean fields. He fell in love with her, and the town, for all the things that made them so different. Since he began urging Nathan to join him. The necessity of circumstance, it seems, finally won.

*****

6:30 Monday morning.

"Hogan, c'mon. We have to clock in by seven. I don't want you to be late your first day."

Uncle Ben patted his nephew's shoulder as he got up from the breakfast table.

"Now, don't look so worried. I already told Mr. Crenshaw what a hard worker you are. All you have to do now is show him."

Hogan took a last bite of bacon then eased over to the counter to retrieve the lunch bag Mommy fixed for him. His stomach churned with nervous anxiousness, thinking how he might not be able to eat any lunch.

Mommy met her son at the other side of the table. She took hold of his arm and squeezed it reassuringly. "You'll do just fine," she told him. "Just listen to the boss man real careful and do just what he says."

Hogan nodded in obedience and hugged Mommy hard before heading out the door behind his uncle.

As they came to the gate of the cannery, Hogan thought how all the people looked like soldiers walking in straight lines. He trembled at the thought of joining a line with so many people he didn't know. Uncle Ben worked in another part of the factory. He would not be able to see him during the day.

Passing through the huge double doors, Hogan lost his breath for the second it took to cross the threshold. As if entering another world, the timid, young man looked around a room that seemed to have no end. Supported by vast wooden beams and concrete walls, it felt cold, damp, and smothering.

"It's always cold first thing in the morning," Ben said, noticing the chill bumps on Hogan's arms. "But don't get too used to it. Things will heat up soon enough."

"Who you got there?" asked a voice from behind.

Hogan and Ben turned to see an odd-looking fellow grinning a wry toothless grin through a shaggy beard, which dripped with tobacco juice.

"This here's my nephew, Hogan," Ben answered reluctantly. "He's come to work in packing. Hogan, this is Duck."

Hogan nodded a shy hello with his head down to not make eye contact.

"Well," Duck began, sloppily spitting his wad of tobacco in a trashcan. "He looks mighty big. But he acts soft. We might just have to toughen him up."

"He don't need a thing from you," Ben warned. "Let's go, Hogan. We have to get your work papers done."

The two walked on down the hall with the chilling sound of Duck's evil laugh floating over their heads.

"Why did you sound so hateful to him?" Hogan asked. "He makes me think of Uncle Whick."

"Maybe so," Ben replied. "And just like Whick, he is full of trouble. You best mark my word and stay clear of that one."

Hogan thought about it as they walked. He never understood why everyone back home thought so badly of Whick. As far as he could see, his great uncle was always a lot of fun. Hogan remembered Whick riding up on his horse to take him on a surprise trip. Mommy always got so mad.

Before he could finish his thinking, they arrived at the factory office. The lady that helped with his papers smiled nicely, and Hogan noticed how pretty she was.

Mr. Crenshaw patted him on the back and said, "Welcome to Morgan's Cannery." The factory manager led his newest employee down another hall to the packing line, where his supervisor, and his new way of life, waited.

"Meet Hogan Watts, fresh from the hills of Kentucky." Mr. Crenshaw announced to Jim Wilson. "He's real green. So start him on the line slow and stay close 'til he gets the hang of things."

"Sure thing, Boss," Wilson spoke loudly in order to hear above the noise of the machinery. "Glad to meet you, Watts," he said to Hogan, reaching out a sweaty hand. "You ready to pack some cans?"

Hogan had no idea what the men were talking about. But he thought they must be awfully friendly as he listened to their hearty laughter.

Mr. Crenshaw talked privately to Wilson for a minute before he slipped out the large swinging doors.

"What ya got there?" Wilson asked, pointing at Hogan's paper bag.

Nearly forgetting that he had been carrying it, Hogan lifted the bag then looked back at his boss man, who waited for an answer.

"It's my lunch, Sir. Mommy made it for me."

"Well, if that ain't sweet," said Wilson sarcastically. "There's a break room around the corner. You can put it in there. Lunch break is at noon for thirty minutes. Keep a close eye on the time, 'cause being late could get you canned."

Wilson chuckled briefly at his joke that Hogan obviously did not get. Clearing his throat, he continued. "The bathroom is next to the break room. You can take a leak when you need to. But you better not need to very often."

Hogan tried hard to pay attention like Mommy told him to. But Mr. Wilson talked so fast he began to feel overwhelmed.

"Listen up," the boss said gruffly. "This is our busy season. Local farmers are bringing in green beans faster than our ladies down the hall can swap recipes. Every day we have to get those beans in cans and on the trucks for shipping. Your job will be down here at the end of the line."

From out of nowhere, a loud spurt of steam rushed out in the air. Workers at the other end scrambled for a release valve. The mixture of wild commotion and shrill blasts from a warning siren froze Hogan in his tracks as Mr. Wilson screamed orders.

"Boys! What do you think you are doing?! Get the temperature gauge set back before you blow us all to kingdom come! You better pray that batch of cans didn't bust, or I'll have your heads on a silver platter!"

Some of the words Mr. Wilson shouted Hogan had only heard one other time. It was at a wedding party back home when two of the Noble brothers got in a terrible fight. Their brawl ended up smashing a table of food and led outside, where one of them wound up dead from a gunshot blast to the chest. Mommy and Daddy took them home almost as soon as it began. But Mommy later warned that too much of the shine had caused their bad end.

Gradually, the workers gained control of the industrial-sized pressure cooker, and Mr. Wilson returned to finish training.

"Now, this is what you'll be doing all day." Mr. Wilson told Hogan, acting as though nothing had just happened.

He demonstrated how to take the freshly sealed cans from a conveyor belt and stack them in slotted wooden crates. Then he lifted the crates onto a hand truck and showed Hogan to the loading dock where he would load the crates in the back of a tractor-trailer truck. To Hogan, it looked very much like a combination bus and pickup truck.

"You have to keep a steady pace, so nothing gets backed up, and everything goes out on time, see?" Mr. Wilson explained and handed Hogan a brown pair of cloth gloves. "You'll want to wear these, or else you'll be picking splinters out of your hands all night. These wooden crates can be hell."

The boss stopped for a moment, looking rather seriously at the tall, well-built young man in front of him.

"There's just one more thing," he said, pulling Hogan away from the rest of the crew. "A lot of the guys you're working with here are some rough characters. Most of them won't bother you. They just want to get the job done and get home, same as the rest of us. But some would just a soon spit on you as look at you. What I'm trying to say is it would be better if you didn't talk to them about your "Mommy." They'd see that as a sign of weakness. Then I'm afraid you'd be fair game for all kinds of meanness."

Hogan didn't understand at all. Didn't these "characters" have mommies? Why would they be mean about something like that? Still, it was Mommy who told him to do what his boss man said. So he agreed with a nod of his head and a quiet, "Yes, Sir."

"Good," said Mr. Wilson in confirmation. "Well, let's get to work. If you need anything, I'll be in my office."

For the rest of the day, Hogan kept very much to himself. He developed games in his mind that helped maintain a rhythm of stacking and loading, which gave him speed. One, two, three, four; one, two, three, four; over and over, he counted cans until several crates were filled. Then he stacked the crates on the hand truck and pushed it down to the loading dock.

In a way, the work reminded him a lot of cutting and stacking wood and fence mending. Daddy taught him to take his chores in small steps. Then before you know it, the job would be done. Soon, he began to feel a certain amount of confidence and pride at the thought of receiving money for a job he could do well.

Mr. Wilson also seemed pleased. He checked on Hogan several times during the day, always with an encouraging, "good job," or "keep up the good work," followed by a kind hand laid on Hogan's shoulder. Generally, however, his next stop at the other end of the line resulted in cursing and shouting orders at the men that Hogan could not quite understand.

*****

During the first few weeks, while Hogan continued to adjust to his working routine, the rest of the family dealt with their own new environment. In between all the discoveries of new ways and searching for an affordable house to rent, they all pitched in at harvesting Aunt Jean's garden.

Jean thrilled at having so much help. Working together made the chore seem like child's play. Even though it wasn't nearly the volume Mommy and Daddy were accustomed to handling; Jean said they could manage through the winter just fine. Soon, the pantry was filled once again with pretty jars of corn, beans, tomatoes, and pickles stacked neatly in rows. Mommy even showed Jean her favorite recipe for chow-chow.

One day each week, the women and girls made a trip to the grocery store. It was such an easy walk to town that Mommy enjoyed herself immensely. Allie and Pearlie Sue also noticed a spring in her step they had not recognized before. Pulling a wagon on this journey felt more like a pleasure trip. It was only a couple of miles to town, and there were no hills to speak of, no winding creek to follow, and no worrying whether they could handle the load all the way back. They could hardly believe that going to town only took the morning and not the whole day.

Downtown Austin consisted of two long rows of connected stores with a street down the middle. The girls watched intently as people flowed in and out of the stores, carrying bags of goods and looking completely happy. Everywhere they turned, examples of a life they nearly missed passed by in front of them.

In one store window, they watched nice looking ladies, wearing pink dresses topped with white aprons, bring plates of breakfast, and pour cups of coffee for people seated at square kitchen tables. Aunt Jean said that was a restaurant, and the ladies were called waitresses. How odd, they thought, to actually pay someone money to cook and bring your food?

Another building housed the department store. To Allie, it was like looking at a Sears & Roebuck Catalogue come to life. Everything you could imagine sat on a shelf or hung on a rack right there in the store. All you had to do was pick it up and buy it. Even though she had no money, Allie imagined herself at the counter, telling the gentleman the list of things she wanted and for him to "wrap them up right away."

"Window shopping can be a wonderful thing," said Aunt Jean, describing the typical behavior of her nieces, whose noses were so close to the glass their breath could be seen. "That's what we call it anyway. It doesn't cost a thing, and it's almost as much fun – to look in and pretend you are just about to walk in and buy whatever your heart desires."

"I just did that," Allie admitted out loud.

"Me too," Pearlie Sue chimed in. "You see that beautiful yellow dress right there?"

"That'll be enough for one day," broke in Mommy, not wanting her daughters to get caught up in material things. "We best get back home with these groceries."

"Not just yet," Jean argued. "I have a little extra change. I'd like to buy us a cherry coke down here at the drug store soda fountain."

"Oh, Jean. You really needn't…."

"Nonsense. Let me do this. We all deserve a treat now and then. Come on. It'll be fun."

Jean took a grinning Allie and Pearlie Sue by the hand, with Sissy following close behind. Mommy shook her head and reluctantly pulled the wagon to catch up as her companions swung open the door of the Austin Drug Store on the corner.

It was the most fascinating place of all, sort of a combination department store and restaurant. Allie gazed from one side where a man stood high above a counter filling tiny bottles with different liquids and tablets, to rows of shelves in the middle laden with trinkets, books, and cards, to the other wall where a lovely lady sat behind a showcase of makeup.

More impressive still was the soda fountain snack bar at the back of the building. The new girls in town soaked in every fantastic sight. The countertop, made of shiny wood, practically sparkled as Pearlie Sue ran her fingers over the grain and marveled at how smooth. "No splinters," she thought.

To the front of the long counter, odd-looking chairs with three tall legs and round seats waited to be occupied. Behind the counter sat the biggest stove they had ever seen. Its gleaming chrome color sizzled along with the different types of meat that lay cooking on the top. To the left of the stove, a strange-looking metal contraption featuring several nozzles and levers generated a calm humming sound.

"What'll it be?" asked the young man from his post behind the bar. He flashed a gleaming smile through a bit of a high-pitched voice, even for a young man.

"Five cherry cokes please," Aunt Jean replied, taking a seat beside Sissy on one of the stools."

Hoping not to appear dumb, the sisters quickly followed suit while keeping a close eye on the fellow mixing their refreshments. They stared in amazement as he reached beneath the counter to retrieve five large-handled glasses. In one swift motion, he dunked the glasses into an ice bucket then plunked them under the machine where he worked the nozzles in an entertaining fashion to produce a dark-colored, fizzing concoction that boasted an inch of foam on top. One at a time, he carefully placed the drinks in front of the ladies.

"That'll be a buck-twenty-five," he announced to Jean, who reached into her change purse and pulled out five quarters. "Thank you very much," he responded politely as she laid the coins in his hand. "Enjoy."

Allie merely watched her treat for a moment. The fizzy bubbles danced and burst into tiny wet particles that tickled her nose with each attempt to take a sip. After a few gulps, she thought how odd it seemed for such a sweet drink to feel as though it burned her throat on the way down.

They all savored each swig, knowing it would be a long time until they would taste another.

Just then, four local teenagers burst into the store. Two handsome boys and two beautiful girls joked and laughed their way toward the soda fountain. They made such a spectacle that Pearlie Sue expected someone to give them a good scolding at any moment.

Allie tried to watch them without being noticed. The boys wore blue jeans and white t-shirts with the sleeves rolled up to their shoulders. By their side, two blonde-haired girls practically danced with richness. From their neatly tailored blouses to their elaborately embroidered poodle skirts, Allie looked them up and down with a hint of envy. Soft, straight hair pulled back in a ponytail bounced as daintily as dandelion petals floating off on a breeze each time the girls threw their pretty heads back in uncontrollable giggles.

Allie and Pearlie Sue drank in the sight of kids having fun, along with the final sips of their cherry coke. They couldn't begin to think of how to have fun like that, not to mention that it was never allowed. Such behavior was considered rude and disrespectful.

To Allie, the whole town did not seem real. It was like watching one of those movie pictures that Sissy told them about. These kids surely had never slopped hogs or rocked chickens out of the garden. She could not imagine they had ever walked barefoot up a craggy hillside to bring cows back to the barn or hoed in a corn patch 'til their hands blistered and bled. How could such joy come from a kid who had never consoled their mother while their little sister lay deathly ill from scarlet fever or the heartbreak of taking up for their older brother who could never take up for himself?

In Lost Creek, people lived ridges apart. They never saw each other except at church, school, and a few special occasions. Yet, they knew every family and all there was to know about them. And no matter how much quibbling went on between them, whenever a bell rang, a helping hand soon followed.

Allie wondered how it could be that all the people in Austin lived so close to each other and seemed so much like strangers. Sure, these kids act like the best of friends, and everyone she sees on the street speaks a polite hello. But something was missing. She didn't seem to feel anything from them.

Suddenly, she felt sadness in the pit of her stomach to realize she was in Austin to stay. This was her home now, whether it felt like it or not. Sadness turned to sinking despair as she worried that she might never belong here among all these pretty people with all their strange things and stranger ways.

"We best get these groceries home," Mommy announced and finished the last swallow of her drink. "Nathan will be wanting his dinner soon."

Aunt Jean looked at the clock on the wall. It read 11 o'clock.

"I guess you're right. Let's go, girls."

One by one, five mugs clanked down on the counter. The Watts women quietly slipped down from the stools and walked single file out of the store. In the process, Allie noticed the teenage clique staring at them and whispering. The sinister sound of their laughter rang with an obvious cruelty.

"They're seniors, you know," Sissy told Allie while on the way home. "They make fun of everybody. They think it's their duty," she said, rolling her eyes at the thought.

"What duty?" asked Pearlie Sue. She had only heard that word in connection with men going off to war.

"I just mean they think because they're older, they can be as mean as they want to, and it's supposed to be fun," Sissy clarified.

"That's not nice at all," stated Pearlie Sue with indignation. Now she knew someone really should give them a good scolding. "I don't want to go to school with seniors."

"Now, don't fret," Mommy broke in, having heard enough of such a conversation. "You have plenty of time to make friends before you get to high school. And I'm sure there are plenty of nice folks too."

"Yeah," Sissy agreed. "And don't forget. One day you'll get to be a senior."

Allie remained quiet the whole walk home, thinking she may not ever fit in. But she knew for certain she would never think being mean was fun, senior or not. Even though church wasn't held every Sunday back home, Mommy made sure they read from the Bible every day. And the "Golden Rule" was etched in their brains from the moment of first memory.

"Do unto others as you would have others do unto you."

Allie doubted that these kids even knew the words. She also sadly wondered if the Jacksons back home thought about it when they lied and sent her family to this strange new world.

*****

In the week before school began, the newest Watts Family in Austin prepared to move into a house of their own. Ben found it from a listing of houses for rent on the bulletin board at the cannery. A tiny two-bedroom house on the other side of town, it needed a lot of work. And the neighborhood wasn't nearly as nice as where Ben and Jean lived. But Hogan could easily afford the amount, so Mommy and Daddy decided they could all make do.

That Saturday, Daddy and Ben borrowed a large pickup truck to haul the rest of their belongings back from Kentucky. Allie went with them because Mommy said she would keep a good eye on things.

Three travelers sweltered under the glaring sun through the windshield. Daddy remarked of how the Dog Days of Summer had settled in. Even the air blowing through open windows felt thick and suffocating. Allie wished they could somehow bring everything back on a bus like they rode on the first trip.

When they finally arrived in Jackson, it was nearly suppertime, and the sandwiches Mommy packed for them were gone. Daddy and Ben determined they had enough gas money to get back with a bit of change to spare for a meal.

Ben turned the truck into a parking space square in front of the restaurant next to the bank building. As hot and tired as she was, Allie still wriggled with anticipation at the thought of eating at a restaurant where a waitress brings your plate and keeps your glass filled.

They each had a plate of chicken and dumplings with green beans and mashed potatoes, and a dinner roll served on a separate plate. Allie enjoyed every bite. However, she couldn't help but wonder why they didn't go on to Grandma Annie's for supper and to spend the night.

Her answer came when they drove by her grandparents' house, and no one came out to greet them. They stayed in their old cabin, which smelled musty from being empty. Allie scarcely slept a wink. It just didn't feel right without the rest of the family.

When no one came the next morning to help with loading or even to see them one last time, Allie finally realized that it didn't feel right to be back in Kentucky at all. She felt lost in the woods, not knowing which way was home. It wasn't here anymore. If she didn't belong here and she didn't belong there, how would she ever survive?

*****

Mommy scrubbed the new house all weekend with bleach water and ajax. She rather liked the linoleum floor in the kitchen and bathroom. There were no cracks for dirt to hide, and it felt smooth and clean after a good mopping. She wished this linoleum covered the floors in the rest of the house. But in the living room, she spread out a large braided rug that Grandma Annie had made for her years ago. Scrap pieces of material salvaged from dressmaking were woven tightly in a colorful round pattern. It brightened the room and made Mommy feel more at home.

After Hogan left for work on Monday, the girls prepared for their first day at school. Pearlie Sue easily selected her best frilly dress; pink gingham with lace around the hem and puffy short sleeves. It was too hot for tights, and she didn't have any fancy bobby socks. Still, Pearlie Sue proudly wore the saddle oxfords she had gotten from the mission house last year. Two pink ribbons completed her tautly plaited hair.

"You look mighty pretty," Mommy told her, wringing her hands at the thought of her daughters heading off for the unknown. She worried about Hogan as well, but he seemed to be doing okay at the cannery. Today, it was Allie and Pearlie Sue who faced an uncertain challenge.

Walking out of the bedroom, Allie fidgeted with her dress. "It's so plain looking," she thought, remembering the beautiful poodle skirts worn by the senior girls at the drug store. At least she had pulled her hair back in a ponytail, as best as she could figure to do it.

"I'll make some new dresses," Mommy said, noticing the expression on her daughter's face. "Just as soon as we get extra money for material."

"A skirt?" asked Allie with begging in her voice.

"A skirt?" Mommy repeated.

"I'd like to have a skirt. And maybe we could stitch a poodle on the front."

"Maybe," Mommy answered, a little hesitant.

She wasn't sure she liked the idea of her girls becoming so fond of all the new material things they saw.

"I know we're in a new place now. And there are so many things to want. But things don't make us a family. Don't y'all forget that everything we've always had is just fine."

"Yes'm," the girls answered obediently.

"Now, get going. I don't want to see you tardy. Remember to stand up straight and mind your manners."

They each kissed their mom on the cheek, grabbed a lunch bag, and headed out the door to the sidewalk where a group of other kids was already walking to school.

It was barely breaking daylight, but Allie could tell the kids in front of them were looking back and talking among themselves. She thought it was very ill-mannered. Why couldn't they just try to be friends? After all, she wanted to know as much about them as they wanted to know about her.

Allie walked her little sister to the junior high school building, just up the street from where she would be at the high school. She could tell that Pearlie Sue did not really want to go in.

"It'll be okay," Allie told her. "Just do your work like you did back home at the schoolhouse. Can't none of these kids be any better than you at arithmetic. Just hold your head up, and you'll make friends. You'll see."

Pearlie Sue nodded her head in a silent thank you to her big sister, then inched her way up to the schoolhouse door.

Allie continued to watch until the door swung open and swallowed he sister inside. She had to hurry now to catch up with the rest of the high school crowd as a funny-sounding bell rang out across the sky. Nothing like the loud clang of the cast iron bell Allie grew up hearing; this bell tolled shrill and harsh.

Suddenly, the moment she had dreaded for a solid week was here. Allie braced herself for whatever might happen, then rounded the corner into the school's office to sign in.

"Mr. Harold Burk, Principal," she read from the door before pushing it open to go in.

It was a large room, painted off-white with a row of chairs on one side and a counter dividing it in half. Bulletin boards loaded with papers hung on every wall. An oscillating fan sat at the edge of the counter, rustling the papers with every spin around its creaky base.

On the other side of the counter, a lady sat at a desk typing. Her fingers moved fast and fluidly. Allie became a little dizzy trying to keep her eyes on the lady's movements. At the end of each line, the secretary slapped the top of the typewriter, pushing it back to the beginning before busily typing some more.

Allie continued to watch the woman in silence, lost in the thought that she would love to be a secretary and be able to type that fast. Finally, the woman noticed Allie, and she abruptly stopped her work.

"What can I do for you, Hon," she asked the nervous new face in front of her. "Well, you must be the new girl."

Swinging around in her chair, the secretary got up and walked over to the counter.

"Yes'm," Allie answered her, relieved at not having to explain.

"Now, don't be shy. My name is Miss White. What's yours?"

"Allie. Allie Watts."

"That's right. I have your records right over here. Your mother and aunt filled out your enrollment papers last week. They said your family moved here from Kentucky. Is that right?"

Allie nodded while sizing up the lady from head to toe. A tall curvaceous woman, she walked gracefully in navy blue, high-heel pumps. Her dress matched the shoes and her curves perfectly, with full petticoats that rustled from beneath. The top of her dress scooped down toward her bosoms. Her light brown hair was done up in a kind of bun that Allie did not recognize.

"Well, it's a good thing they finally got you out of there and up here in a real civilization," Miss White continued. "I just hope it's not too late. You did some good work in school down there. But you're missing a lot of classes that are required for college."

As Miss White kept talking, Allie wondered what she meant by a "real civilization." Still, the nice secretary made her feel at ease, and she wished she could stay in the office and not go to class at all.

"Here is your schedule. You have six different classes, and there are five minutes between each one. You know, Hon." Miss White hesitated briefly. "You have study hall first period. I could use some help around here – filing, making copies for the teachers, things like that. If you want, I'll talk to Mr. Burk about letting you come here every morning instead of going to study hall. I think it would be good for you. Would you like that?"

It was as if she had read Allie's mind, and she couldn't help but smile at her good fortune.

"Yes, Ma'am." She answered, nodding gleefully and wondering at the same time how Pearlie Sue was doing at her school.

"Now see. You do have a pretty smile. We'll just have to get you to talk more and maybe do something about that wild head of hair."

Miss White reached across the counter and fiddled with Allie's ponytail.

"I bet if you rolled it up on great big curlers at night, it would straighten right out."

A grimace instantly replaced Allie's smile. She had hoped no one would call attention to how different she looked. She felt self-conscious enough already.

"Oh, I'm sorry, Hon," Miss White apologized. "I didn't mean to hurt your feelings. I know that's the hair God gave you. But he never said we couldn't make it look better. That's why he gave us the ability to curl and tease. Besides," she said with a wink and a hushed voice, "men around here love a head full of soft, straight hair on a woman. You do want to attract the boys, don't you?"

Taken-a-back, Allie literally did not know how to answer. She had never thought about attracting anything, except maybe small animals and, of course, hummingbirds.

Just then, Mr. Burke came out to meet his new pupil. A large man with thick eyebrows, and a thicker mid-section, the principal stared down at Allie with intimidating eyes. After a moment of introductions, he announced intentions of showing Allie around to her classes.

"Be so kind as to type these letters while I'm gone, Miss White. Allie can begin helping you with light duties first thing in the morning."

Taking the notepad from her boss's hand, Miss White threw a wink in Allie's direction before returning to her typewriter and the blissful clinking noise it made.

Drab gray walls tunneled as far as she could see. Their monotony was broken only by a few notice-filled bulletin boards and banners dressed in black and white to hail the school's beloved Austin Eagles.

Door after door, they passed by in silence. Allie's ragged saddle oxfords were squeaking with each step across the shiny tile floor. How would she ever find her way back? What if all the kids were like the ones she saw at the drug store soda fountain?

Queasiness lingered in the pit of Allie's stomach as they turned down yet another hallway. She eased her eyes upward to look at Principal Burk walking beside her. He returned the glance but continued his pace toward the large double doors just ahead.

"This is your second-period class, PE," Mr. Burk announced in a monotone voice, his large stature shifting to retrieve a piece of paper from a file he carried under his arm.

Allie peered at him in complete innocence, a thousand questions hiding behind dark, unknowing eyes.

"Here is your daily schedule," he said bluntly, handing her the slip of paper. "Each day, after aiding Miss White in the office, you will come here. Then you will have math, science, world geography, and home economics."

Allie's blank expression brought his instructions to a halt.

"If there is something you don't understand, now is the time to ask," he prompted.

Studying the face of this particular elder, Allie could not detect any sign of emotion. She saw nothing especially mean or kind in the way he awaited an answer.

"What is PE and home economics?" she finally asked, worried that he would think she was stupid.

"Ah, yes. I suppose you wouldn't be familiar with such classes."

Principal Burk situated himself in an all-knowing stance, crouching slightly to make sure his ignorant new student had full view of his authority.

"Firstly, home economics gives young ladies the basics of cooking, how to maintain a nice home, and proper etiquette. PE stands for physical education. It is a class for students to get some exercise and to learn how to stay healthy."

His explanations seemed a bit confusing to Allie, a class just to exercise and one to teach cooking? What a waste of time, she thought. These are things she already learned at home from Mommy.

"I realize you are not accustomed to a daily routine such as this." Mr. Burk concluded in response to her apparent lack of understanding. "However, you will find that learning proper behaviors and speech will be to your advantage in the future. I do not tolerate phrases like "y'all" and "over yonder." You will be much better off once you have put the old Kentucky ways behind."

The principal's speech did not sit well with Allie. She felt her gut tighten with resentment. What did he know about the "old Kentucky ways?" And just maybe, she thought, these people in Austin could learn a thing or two from them.

Still, because of her upbringing, she held her tongue and mustered up only a polite, "Yes, Sir."

Inside the gymnasium, Allie felt like an ant inside a jar. It looked big enough to hold all the houses in Lost Creek. Every sound reverberated through each wall and back again; the echoing mixed with Allie's heart beating in her ears. She felt as though she might actually collapse from sheer nervousness. Still, she walked on toward the rest of the class seated on bleachers at the other side of the huge room.

Miss Mills, the gym teacher, welcomed Allie and instructed her to take a seat beside the rest of the girls. But Allie didn't feel very welcome. Searing eyes felt like a burning in her flesh, though she dared not look in their direction. Short, muffled giggles hurt her feelings terribly.

Her eyes were fixed on her own fidgeting saddle oxfords. Suddenly, she believed she knew how the hummingbird felt to be trapped in the oatmeal box while she carried him around, showing everyone that she really caught him. She thought about how his tiny wings beat furiously, fluttering and pecking in desperation to be set free.

"Girls, Pay attention!" Miss Mills ordered. "You will need to know these things if you expect to pass this class."

Allie strained to hear every word. She certainly did not want to look dumb in front of the other girls, even if she did think the whole idea of PE was silly.

Miss Mills looked very comfortable, walking back and forth on the gymnasium floor. She wore a white tee shirt and black, baggy pants of some sort. Her hair was pulled up in a tight bun, and she carried a whistle around her neck, which she often blew "just for demonstration."

At the end of class, another bell sounded, causing all the girls to jump up and hurry out of the gym. Miss Mills shouted final instructions at them as they continued walking and laughing. Only one other girl besides Allie lagged behind.

"Hi, my name's Teresa," she told Allie, bearing a pleasant grin. "Are you really a Kentuckian?"

"Uh-huh," Allie answered, nodding her head in confirmation as the two proceeded out into the hall.

"I've never made friends with a Kentuckian before. But you seem really nice. I guess I haven't been in class with any either. There aren't that many of you around. Mostly I just see them coming in and out of town. Do you live in the Kentuckian neighborhood behind the cannery?"

Allie listened to the girl ramble on as she examined her soft, brown hair tied in a silky, pink scarf and the fluffy matching poodle skirt that rippled around as she spoke.

"You know, it's only been a few years that you people have been allowed to come to this school," Teresa informed Allie nonchalantly.

"Why?" Allie questioned harshly, an eyebrow raised in disbelief.

"Oh. Well, they went to the old Austin school on Oak Street," Teresa replied a little off-guard. "My dad said they had to go there because none of them could pass the tests. And besides, he said it was really better for them to be with their own kind. You know, so they wouldn't feel out of place."

Completely stunned, Allie could not believe what she heard. This girl talked about her people as if they were lepers that needed to be kept away from decent folk "for their own good." Worse still, she didn't seem to see anything wrong in what she said. But Allie held back her thoughts because she so wanted to fit in and Teresa at least acted like she wanted to be friends.

"Anyway," Teresa continued. "You are mighty dark-skinned."

The new Hoosier acquaintance stopped to look over all of Allie's features.

"And look how black and curly your hair is! Say, are you a Negro from Kentucky?"

Now Allie didn't know if she wanted to be friends with this girl. Flushed with embarrassment, she crossed her brown arms tightly and wished one of them would disappear.

"No!" Allie shot back, knowing enough from lessons about the Civil War to know how Black people are treated.

At least her ancestors weren't beaten and locked up as slaves. Maybe that's why it was always common knowledge that it was better to be a dark hillbilly than a Black person. Regardless, Allie suddenly realized how Black people feel; being judged by the color of their skin.

"Good," Teresa stated, acting relieved. "Cause my dad says Blacks aren't even allowed to live in this county."

"Your dad knows a lot," Allie broke in, desperately wanting to change the subject and feeling that she understood why the other girls had left them behind.

"Yeah. I guess he does. You know, he owns the dress shop in town, next to the drugstore. Well, here's my class. I'll see you tomorrow in gym."

Allie watched Teresa skip across the hall and into the room. Other students whizzed by as she recalled looking into that dress shop window. How lucky Teresa was to not know what it was like to be different, she thought, and to have a father who owned a dress shop.

*****

The next morning, Allie felt much braver about going to school. Surely the worst was behind her now. She even got over the thoughtless remarks of Teresa Johnson, especially after Daddy's talk about giving the people in Austin a chance to get used to us, "same as we have to get used to them."

There were a few more Kentucky kids in Pearlie Sue's school, and she had already made several friends. So the sister walked more briskly down the street, parting ways at the junior high with a hope-filled hug.

"Well, I see you made it back!" Miss White greeted when she saw Allie enter the office. "I've made a list of some things I'd like for you to do. But I suspect we may have to have a lesson on some of the machines around here. Have you ever used a mimeograph machine?"

"No, Ma'am," Allie answered, a little embarrassed.

"Now, don't you worry, Hon. I can tell you're a smart, young lady. You'll get the hang of it in no time."

The secretary was right. Time in the office did pass quickly. Allie marveled at the mimeograph machine. All she had to do was attach a piece of paper to the roller, fill the container with a funny smelling ink, turn the handle, and exact copies came out the other end.

Just as she became a little more at ease, the bell signaled time for her to leave and go to PE class.

"Good work, Hon," Miss White complimented. "I'll see you tomorrow."

Allie reluctantly picked up her books and headed out into the maze of hallways, telling herself over and over that everything was all right. She would be just fine…if she could manage to avoid much conversation with Teresa Johnson.

The gymnasium clattered with all sorts of activity. On one end of the glossy, wooden floor, the boys' class stood around a tall pole. They each took turns throwing a ball toward the net attached at the top while clapping and shouting at each other. It all seemed so odd to Allie. The only games she knew of were tag and seeing who could hit a rock the farthest with a wooden stick.

"Let's hurry and dress-out!"

Allie finally recognized that Miss Mills was shouting directly at her. She rushed over to the girls' side, where her teacher waited.

"You didn't get your uniform yesterday. So come on, and I'll find one for you."

Miss Mills led Allie into the locker room. Each wall was lined with the same type of book lockers as those in the hallway. In front of the lockers, a row of wooden benches held piles of clothes. The faint aroma of bleach and dirty socks permeated the air.

"Here. This should fit," Miss Mills decided, handing Allie a black and white shorts jumpsuit that buttoned all the way up the front. "You'll take it home with you every day and see that it's washed. Wearing a dirty uniform will knock five points from your grade. Now let's hurry. Class is about to begin."

The gym teacher strutted out, and Allie found herself alone in the dank, odor-filled room. She held the uniform up in front of her. Its length ended just above her knee. Allie was shocked to imagine that such an outfit was considered o.k. to wear at school. Yet, the other girls were already dressed. And after all, she was supposed to get used to their ways.

The young, Melungeon descendant slipped into one of the commode stalls to change. Miss Mills' selection was good. The uniform fit her body perfectly. Her dark skin practically shimmered beneath the black and white fabric. She neatly laid her regular clothes on one of the benches and set out to join the others.

During class, Allie concentrated hard on the lessons at hand so as not to be distracted by the stares and giggles. Unfortunately, Teresa was another matter. She stuck to Allie's side, taking every opportunity to enlighten her new friend with unflattering details about their classmates.

"Suzy, over there, is wearing her hair down this week because she has a hickey on the back of her neck. They say she got it from a boy down in Scottsburg. If her parents knew, they would just die. You'll see. She likes to show it off when the teachers aren't around. And I know for a fact that Melissa smokes cigarettes every chance she gets. My dad said Mr. Barnes, Melissa's dad, was getting mighty fed up with the way she comes home after curfew."

Smiling awkwardly, Allie pretended to follow along with Teresa's stories, though she did not understand half of what she heard. She had no idea what a hickey or curfew was. As for smoking cigarettes, Grandma Annie was the only woman she knew that liked tobacco. Mommy always said it was a bad habit she learned from her brothers, and she didn't want any of her kids to even try it.

"They're just jealous, you know." Teresa babbled on while the group practiced running in place, attempting to make Allie feel better about the mean treatment from the other girls.

"You're really pretty. And your dark skin makes you stand out. They don't like anyone that overshadows them. You see all those guys looking your way?"

Allie made a quick glance in the direction of the boys' class to see several grinning faces staring her way. She shot her head back toward Teresa, feeling a pang of nervous delight.

"Allie and Teresa!" shouted Miss Mills. "The girls' class is over here. I suggest you join us while we choose teams for basketball!"

"Oops," Teresa uttered softly, covering her mouth with her hand and winking at Allie. "Come on." She grabbed Allie's arm, pulling her into line with the others.

The remainder of class was spent practicing the skills of dribbling and passing a basketball while Miss Mills barked orders and blew her whistle. By the end, they were all hot and sweaty. Allie began to wonder if they were allowed to go home and clean up before the next class.

When the bell rang, and Miss Mills shouted to "hit the showers!" the other girls scurried off, talking and laughing. But Allie stood still in confusion.

"Aren't you coming?" asked Teresa.

"Yeah…sure," Allie stammered, following reluctantly.

In the locker room, she heard water running and saw steam billowing out from an open room at the far end. Sounds of talking mixed with intermittent squeals from within.

Inching her way closer to the opening, Allie peered through the doorway to see a group of naked girls standing beneath a row of pipes with water showering down on them. The naïve mountain girl watched in horror as they busily washed, teased, and laughed. Bare breasts and buttocks of every shape and size paraded right in front of her, covered only in a wet, soapy lather.

Feeling faint, Allie turned back toward the locker room, ashamed of what she saw, even more ashamed that she was expected to join them. Her heart pounded and her stomach churned with nausea.

She had never seen a naked body besides her own, not even Pearlie Sue, at least not since she was a little girl taking a bath in front of the fireplace back home. Back home, they were taught about modesty from the moment their bodies began to develop.

"No one is to see those parts of your body 'cept God," Mommy told them. "Nakedness is as great a sin as any."

Allie recalled the last time she saw part of a woman's breast. It was a picture on a calendar that hung over the buffet in Grandma Naomi's kitchen. She remembered vividly the face of a young, beautiful woman smiling as though she were proud to be looked at by whoever was willing. The top of her dress was tight as a corset and scooped way down, revealing two mounds of white flesh pushed as tightly together as nature would allow.

Though she would never admit it, Naomi only wanted the calendar because it was the only thing Lilly left behind on her way to California. But she could not abide the sight of naked bosoms greeting her, or any visitors, in her kitchen. So, one day, during a visit, Naomi instructed Allie to draw in a necklace on the bare part of the picture. And she eagerly obliged, taking her crayons from school and creating an elaborate circle of color until the cleavage disappeared. Allie remembered well the name "Loretta Young" printed in large letters at the bottom. None of them ever knew the lady or why she was important enough to have her name on the bottom of a picture. Maybe one day, they would hear from Lilly, and she could tell them all about it.

For now, Allie sat devastated on the edge of the nearest bench. How could this school allow such a thing? Feeling again like the hummingbird, she prayed she could somehow burst free from this place and fly back home where she felt safe.

"Allie! What are you waiting for?"

Miss Mills came in to check on the girls, who were filing out of the showers, wrapped in towels and preparing to get dressed.

Allie could only look at her teacher with somber eyes; her heart filled with dread.

"What is the matter with you? Don't you know what a shower is?" Miss Mills persisted.

Holding back a floodgate of heavy tears, Allie opened her mouth to respond. "I…not…with everybody," was all she could get out.

"Oh, come now," said Miss Mills.

The teacher took a seat beside her obviously scared student while watching the rest of the class gather up their books. The same talking and laughter trailed to a muffle as they exited the room.

"We are all females here," Miss Mills continued. "We all have the same parts. There's nothing to be ashamed of. I know you're from the backwoods, but surely you can understand that."

Allie wanted to scream. Why does everybody keep saying that the ways of her people are wrong? Why can't they see how wrong they are to her? It's wrong to wash your body in front of other people!

Instead, she simply tugged at her uniform and held her vision steadfast on the tile floor.

"All right," Miss Mills said in finality. "Now that the other girls are gone, you may take this shower in private. I will write a note for your next teacher. But from now on, I expect you to come straight in here and take your shower. If you're going to attend this school, you will have to abide by the same rules as the other students. Otherwise, you will not pass this class. And you must pass this class in order to graduate. Do you understand?"

"Yes, ma'am," Allie answered in the same solemn manner, telling herself over and over that she would not let them break her spirit.

As water from the shower poured over her body, tears flowed with it. Like a fish out of water, she struggled for strength; strength to come to terms with this new way of life; strength to carry on to-day, and strength to endure whatever may come.

"I can never tell Mommy about this," she told herself. "She wouldn't let me finish school. And I have to finish school."

Then she thought about Pearlie Sue. She had to figure out a way to tell her before she got into high school. She couldn't let her sister suffer the same shock. For now, she had no choice but to bear it all in silence.

*****

"Hey, Hogan! Where ya goin', Big Boy?"

The voice came from Duck, who sidled up next to Hogan outside the cannery just after quitting time.

"I'm talkin' to you, Boy. Ain't you got no manners?"

Hogan felt the intimidation, even if he didn't know what to call it. The shabbily dressed, ill-bred coworker's sinister grin dripped with intimidation. Uncle Ben had told him to stay clear of this local, good-for-nothing. But he could see no way around Duck's directness.

"I'm goin' home," Hogan replied meekly.

"Well, well. Goin home to mama – like a good boy."

The harsh, teasing sound in Duck's voice confused Hogan. He made it sound like being good was a bad thing.

Hot, humid air of early fall moved slowly around. Smoke from Duck's cigarette hung heavy as if trapped in the space where they stood. Soon, Hogan could not keep from choking out the strong fumes, all the while noticing other groups of cannery workers gleefully heading home for the night.

"What's the matter, Mama's boy? Never smoked a stogie before? I said you needed toughin' up. Might as well start today."

Nervous and wishing he was home, Hogan struggled to imagine what Duck had in mind. Still, he did want to be tougher. He never told Allie, but he always hated that she did all the fighting for him at school back home. Not that he hated his sister for wanting to protect him. He just hated that he never had the courage to stand up for himself. Yes, it would be nice for people to think he was strong and brave.

"Yeah," Duck continued, "I think it's time you stayed out with the guys. Come on. I know just what you need."

Pleased with himself, this man, ten years Hogan's senior, knew he had gained a follower. "Let's see how happy the boss man is when his favorite boy shows up to work with a hangover," Duck chuckled to himself.

Hogan followed in cautious obedience. Not knowing where they would end up caused a knot to form in the pit of his stomach.

Each step down the sidewalk brought more hesitation and more cajoling from Duck.

"Don't be laggin' behind, Mama's Boy. Tonight you're gonna learn what a man wants from this God-forsaken world. I'm talkin' about pleasure, pure manmade pleasure. The kind you can see with your eyes, touch with your hands, and taste with your tongue."

Duck's wild gestures and excited voice drew Hogan's attention away from his surroundings. Before he knew it, they turned into a narrow alleyway filled with sights and sounds that both frightened and intrigued the naïve youngster from Lost Creek.

Laughing men and women lined both sides of the tiny corridor, which separated the drugstore building and the department store. They all seemed to have a large glass bottle with some sort of drink in it. Every few minutes, someone would say something so funny that another would have to spew out the liquid to keep from choking. Huge, swirling smoke rings hovered just above their heads before dissipating into the evening sky.

Hogan stood motionless, taking it all in until startled by the clanging crash of a metal trash can.

"Hey, you guys!" Duck announced loudly. "This here's Hogan. He's the new hand at the cannery I told you about. And I want you to make him feel really welcome."

He finished with an over-emphasized wink and uproarious laughter from the group. Then he walked to the back of the alley, only to return in a few minutes accompanied by a woman. Hogan thought she was the most beautiful thing he had ever seen. She wore a sleeveless, black dress, which hugged the shape of her slim body and showed leg through a slit way past her knees. Her hair was as white as a January snow. Fluffy and soft-looking, it flowed sensuously over the light skin of her bare shoulders. Her eyes and cheeks were heavily colored with face paint, and a sweet perfume permeated the air around her. But Hogan fixated on the deep, shiny redness of her lips.

"Hogan. Say hello to Gloria." Duck said in a wry introduction. "She's gonna be your date tonight." Turning to Gloria, Duck continued. "That's alright with you, ain't it, Doll Face?"

"Oh yeah," Gloria answered with a delighted squeal. "He's a cutie pie."

Grinning sheepishly, Hogan felt embarrassed by all the attention. His face went flush, and his shoulders drooped. Yet, he kept his eyes on Gloria's lips as she spoke.

"Come on, Big Fella. We're gonna have ourselves a good time."

Hogan supposed this date must be the same as courting back home. Though he always expected his first courtship would be having supper at the girl's house and then sitting on the porch watching the sun go down, just like Mommy described her first courting with Daddy.

Gloria moved closer to Hogan, slipping her arm around his. With her other hand, she raised a bottle to her mouth for a short sip then offered it to her new friend. Hogan politely took the bottle and drank without inspecting the contents. The strong burning sensation instantly reminded him of the moonshine his Uncle Whick used to make.

Uncle Whick always kept a dozen or so bottles stored in his barn. Anytime Hogan helped him chop wood or mend fences, his reward was a man-to-man sip of the shine. Hogan vividly remembered how funny it always made him feel, so strong, so grownup, so normal. He liked that very much. He also liked the feel of Gloria's arm around his so much that he scarcely thought about Mommy's warning of liquor being the devil's drink.

It was too late. He had the taste in his mouth that Duck promised, the beauty of Gloria right in front of him, and the feel of her skin next to his. Hogan believed he had finally found a place in this world where he fit in. His clouded mind allowed him to absorb every experience offered.

"Where are we going?" Hogan asked Gloria as she led him out of the alleyway by his hand.

"My house, so we can be alone. You would like to spend some time alone with me, wouldn't you?"

Hogan nodded shyly, wondering if she had a porch swing.

"Well, let's go," she insisted. "I promise you'll have a real good time."

The two slipped away quietly, leaving the dimly lit alley and the noise of their friends behind.

It was getting late, but Hogan didn't seem to notice. The effect of the alcohol left him oblivious to time or reason or any thought of Mommy and Daddy being worried sick at home. Like a found puppy, he followed his new owner in great anticipation of things to come.

"Here we are," Gloria announced. She skipped up the steps, then turned and motioned for Hogan to follow. A bright glow of the moon caught them at the door, where they stared at each other for a full breathless moment. Gloria's desire for the handsome young man piqued the notion that his willingness may serve to be useful in many ways. Hogan simply wanted to be wanted.

Gloria Foster was a 22-year-old native of Austin and an outcast from her family. Her crime camme as a teenager when she report-ed that her father raped her. No one in town believed Mr. Foster would do such a thing, so she was written off as a hopeless liar.

Since that time, she worked at the cannery by day and found plea-sure where she could at night. Desperate to escape the pain, she allowed her heart to harden. She didn't care about anyone else's feelings or the bad reputation she made for herself among the locals. After all, they never cared about her or the truth of what her wealthy, well-respected father had done. So what did it matter?

Still, her greatest desire was to have someone take care of her. She didn't need to be rich. She'd had that life. But she didn't want someone with a temper like Duck either. This sweet, gentle man in front of her, who had no idea of her past, seemed like just the ticket she needed.

Entering the two-room shanty that Gloria called home, the pair of wayward souls found solace in each other. At first, Hogan resisted when she tried removing his shirt. But the more she kissed him, the less he resisted. Feelings welled up that he was powerless to control. He kissed her back, harder and longer.

"This is wonderful," he thought, taking in all the affection that his drunken mind allowed.

Gloria finished undressing her new lover and sighed wantonly at the sight of his trim, muscular body. She felt as though she could melt into his dark skin and striking, blue eyes. He was magazine gorgeous, and for tonight, he was hers.

Hogan accepted this woman's gift of herself. Her warmth and softness enveloped his every need at that moment. There was no need for thinking. The desire was natural. The feeling was pure bliss. He never wanted it to end.

But daylight came all too soon. Hogan woke with the first break. He rolled over in Gloria's bed to find her sleeping peacefully. With a gentle stroking of her hair and nudging her body, he eventually succeeded in waking her. It was Saturday morning, and his family had no idea where he was. He had to let them know he was o.k., better than o.k.

"Come on, sleepyhead. We have to go," he whispered.

"What are you talking about? It's Saturday. We don't have to go anywhere."

"We have to go see my family. Tell them we're getting married."

"Married?! Are you crazy? I don't know you well enough to get married. I don't even know your last name, for God's sake! And you sure don't know me at all, or you wouldn't even think about marrying me," she protested loudly. "Besides, you're supposed to fall in love or something before you get married."

Shocked and bewildered, Hogan took a few minutes to respond while he watched her throw on some clothes and light up a cigarette.

"I don't know a lot of things," he began slowly. "But it seems to me that you're supposed to get married before doing what we did last night. Seems to me that getting married is the only way to make it right, and my full name is John Hogan Watts."

Gloria studied the determination on his face. Making things right resonated with her. Not the sex part. She didn't care about that. Just making things right in general. Marriage was never an option she expected with anyone. She didn't want to be tied down that way. But Hogan here was so innocent. He wouldn't know what to expect from marriage. She could tell him anything, and he would believe it. And then, if he was willing, a husband is bound to take care of his wife, and that was all she really wanted. Besides, getting married would allow her to get rid of the horrible family name she now hated.

"Well now, Hogan Watts, that actually makes more sense than anything I've heard lately. My name is Gloria Foster, and I'd be pleased to marry you."

"How about that," she thought. "One of Duck's mean pranks has a happy ending."

Hogan swelled with pride, grabbing up his wife-to-be and lifting her off the floor while kissing her like a prized possession.

*****

Allie and Pearlie Sue peered from behind the living room window at children playing on the sidewalk. Some rode by on bicycles, some rolled on roller-skates, while others sat in a circle playing jacks. They all seemed to have such a good time. The Watts girls longed to join them. But Mommy wouldn't hear of it. She was too fearful of everything in this new world. Already, her son was missing, and she couldn't bear the thought of her girls getting hurt or becoming corrupted.

For now, Mommy rustled around in the kitchen, cleaning up breakfast dishes while worriedly gazing down the street. A knock at the door interrupted her deep prayer. Without thinking, she dropped the dishtowel and hurried to see who it was.

"Have you heard anything yet? Is he home?" asked Aunt Jean, whisking through the doorway in hopes of hearing good news.

Mommy shook her head and retreated back to the kitchen. She picked up the towel to begin drying dishes again as if keeping busy would keep bad news from coming.

"Try not to worry, Lottie. I'm sure Ben and Nathan will find him," said Jean, trying to console her friend while convincing herself that everything would be all right.

At that moment, the kitchen door swung open again. This time it was Nathan and Ben. The looks on their faces told the women enough. Hogan was still out there somewhere.

Nathan hugged his sobbing wife, gently leading her to the living room to sit down. Everyone cried and embraced, asking God "why?" and begging him to bring their loved one home.

Allie, especially, could not understand what would keep her brother from coming home. After all the roaming around the hills and woods back home, how could he possibly get lost in this town?

Just then, the eldest Watts girl noticed a shadow moving through the kitchen. She gasped, and the rest of the family rushed to see. Through tearful eyes, they peered at the prodigal son standing in the kitchen with his arm around a strange woman.

Looking over the pair in disbelief, they noticed Hogan's un-combed hair, his untucked shirt, and the embarrassed way he looked back at them. As for his companion, all they saw was a no-good woman with a painted-up face, dyed white hair, hips molded into pink pedal pushers, and a tight white top.

"Hogan, Son, where in the world have you been?" Daddy asked sternly. "Don't you know we've been afraid you were dead?"

Mommy stood back in silence, wringing her hands in the apron around her waist, trying hard not to think what this painted-up floozy might want with her eldest child.

"I-I've been with Gloria," Hogan told them. He instantly sensed the disapproval in the room and wished he were smart enough to explain exactly how he felt.

"We're gonna get married," he announced. "I'm a man. It's time I had my own family."

A moment of dead silence gave way to Mommy retreating in tears. Uncle Ben and Aunt Jean sat in shock while anger churned inside Daddy.

"Girls, go to your room. I want to have a talk with your brother."

Too scared not to, Allie and Pearlie Sue did as they were told. Though filled with curiosity, they knew this was something bad and did not want to be in the middle. Allie couldn't help but think about other times when Hogan did things she thought were dumb. One time, he chopped two whole oak trees that Daddy had cut down the evening before. Without asking, he worked all day splitting and stacking that wood. Allie understood that her broth-er only wanted to be praised for doing a good job. But Daddy was furious to find the trees he wanted for lumber chopped into pieces. It was painfully obvious to Allie that Hogan had trouble thinking things through. But when he made up his mind to do something, he put his whole heart into it.

"Boy, you don't know enough about getting married. You don't know enough about this girl," Daddy accused.

"Yes, sir, I do," Hogan began in defense of his decision. "I know I love Gloria, and I want to take care of her like you take care of Mommy and all of us."

Daddy sat at the table, scratching his head in frustration.

"But I knew your mother for a long time before I knew I wanted to be married. Being married is for the rest of your life. I'm just trying to tell you that it'd be a shame to marry the wrong one."

"Yes, sir, I know." Hogan defended again, stopping short of telling his father the intimate details of how he came to make such a hasty decision. "Gloria is the right one, so I know we should get married."

Daddy had never seen his son so determined, not merely from the words he spoke, but from the surety in his stance and a deepness in his voice that seemed to appear overnight. Still, it was Hogan's eyes that gave Daddy great concern. He knew the eyes of guilt. He knew the pain caused by following guilt rather than seeking what was truly right. And he doubted his son's ability to know the difference. Saddest of all, he knew there was nothing more he could do to stop it.

"Don't worry, Mr. Watts," said Gloria. "Me and Hogan will be fine." She tried her best to sound genuine, though she fidgeted, uneasy to be in a home so obviously filled with love and concern.

A suspicious eye was Daddy's only response to his future daughter-in-law before leaving the room to comfort his sobbing wife.

Gloria looked around the room. It was all so neat and tidy, from the polished wooden table Daddy made to the perfectly scrubbed counters to the sparkling clean linoleum floor. She marveled at how she could envy such a modest home in one of the poorest neighborhoods in town. Still, it was better than where she lived. And even though she knew Hogan would never have much money, he did have a steady paycheck. For Gloria, anyone else's money was better than having to work for herself.

"Come on, Hoagie," she finally said, tugging on his huge bicep. "Let's go get hitched."

*****

Hogan felt elated. Blinded by the physical joys of marriage and a false sense of manhood, he carried himself with pride such as he had never known. He knew full well that he was proud; proud of being a husband, proud of being loved by such a beautiful woman, and proud of becoming the head of his own home. It felt so good.

He just couldn't make sense of how it could be so sinful to feel that way.

The newlywed couple moved into one of the rental houses owned by the Cannery. Better than Gloria's old shanty, the one-bedroom dwelling still wasn't much. But Hogan beamed to carry his bride through the narrow doorway.

Each week, the amount of rent was deducted from his pay. The rest he gave to Gloria. It was easy enough to convince her naïve husband that she needed to have the money to spend on groceries and household goods while he was at work.

For a time, the routine seemed to work. Hogan was so happy to be married that he never noticed what little housekeeping Gloria did or how bare the cabinets were. It never occurred to him that the money was always gone or that his wife spent more time away from home. All that mattered was her being with him each evening, giving him just enough attention to keep his love and trust.

Talk about town may have quelled, but Mommy still was not convinced. What could this no-good woman want with her son, who is so meek and unworldly?

"She's gonna hurt my boy," Mommy would say to Daddy, who always replied in a soothing voice.

"You have to let him be, Lottie. He has to find his own way."

By now, Nathan had become well enough to work again. Lottie liked to believe it was the warm herbal rubs she applied to his back each evening, mixed with God's good grace that healed her husband's crippling pain. In any event, her heart thrilled to see him take up the carpenter's work he always loved.

Hanging around the local lumber mill, Nathan heard of several jobs that needed to be done. Word of this Kentuckian's craftsmanship spread quickly until his building and remodeling services were in full demand.

Soon, he was able to afford a more modern lifestyle for his family. But Lottie refused most of the "new-fangled" gadgets. She wouldn't hear of replacing her old wringer washing machine with a new powered one. It couldn't possibly clean good enough. An electric iron was simply a waste when her heavy cast iron one still worked fine. And why would she want to plug in a noisy mixer? Her egg white icing always came out nice and fluffy with the hand crank beaters Grandma Annie gave her years ago.

One thing the whole family agreed on was a small, tabletop model television set. Allie and Pearlie Sue giggled with glee the day Daddy brought it home in his new 1957 Chevrolet. As their parents situated the box in the living room, they watched in anticipation and prepared to turn it on.

Maybe now they would get to see some of what their friends at school talked so much about. They laughed about a show where three little guys ran around hitting each other all the time called "The Three Stooges" and another about a funny lady named

Lucy. But the most talk centered around each week's singing star on "The Ed Sullivan Show." However, their excitement tinged slightly to hear that the rules would be the same as with the radio. They would only be able to watch "The Grand Ole Opry" each week. Mommy and Daddy watched the evening news broadcast, but "None of that foolishness will be watched in this house."

The "Opry" was even grander to watch than to hear. The girls marveled at the stunning gowns worn by Patsy Cline and Loretta Lynn. They almost felt the facial expressions of each singer who seemed to float across the stage. Even Mommy's foot tapped a little lighter when the bluegrass band came on to pick "Rocky Top."

Hearing "Rocky Top" always made Lottie long for home, just a little. One Sunday morning, after praying and worrying about Hogan, she thought of how long it had been since they were at a church meeting. She dearly missed the fellowship of her kinfolk, closing her eyes to imagine intermittent "Hallelujahs!" Then she heard in her mind a rendition of "Just as I am" being lined by Mrs. Fugate. The centuries-old practice began with one person of the congregation leading the song by speaking one line at a time, then joining in with the tune. The "liner" had to be talented with rhythm to keep up and keep the congregation on track.

But Lottie had a nervous nature, especially around strangers. Whether an inborn condition or the result of ancestral conditioning, she could never bring herself to attend a local church service. No one from Austin, other than family members, would ever be more than a stranger. So she contented herself to be home. Sometimes she went with Nathan to see a house he was building or went to the grocery store with Jean.

This particular Sunday morning, the Lost Creek girl's heart yearned for something. Strangely drawn to the television set, her hand trembled to turn the knob. As though by miracle, a man appeared on the screen.

Standing behind a solid wooden pulpit, he spoke loudly, shaking a Bible in his right hand for emphasis. Lottie stood in quiet disbelief, listening to his words as thankful tears streamed from her eyes. She simply knew with all her heart that God put this preacher on the television just for her.

*****

"Man, Hogan! What's with you?"

Gloria stomped through the house, kicking off her shoes and pulling off her clothes.

"I hang around this dump all day. I wash your clothes. I even try to cook something sometimes. Hell, I've never done that for anybody. Now, I wanna go out and have some fun!"

Hogan stood bewildered, watching his wife change into a fancy, new red dress. It showed the curves of her figure well, as tresses of satiny, straight blonde hair glided down her back. The thought of other men looking at her that way upset Hogan. Yet, he feared upsetting Gloria more. She could be cruel.

"Besides," Gloria said while putting on makeup. "I don't say anything when you go over to your mom's all the time. You're supposed to be the big man now. Look at you. You can't even keep up with your wife."

A puzzled expression came over Hogan's face. In plain thought, he just didn't know where else to go for food. She rarely kept any in their house, nor did she allow him to keep any money in his pocket.

"I just want you to be home with me – be my wife, like you promised."

"Don't you get all pitiful on me!" Gloria ordered. "You get to be with your friends at work all day. Well, I miss my friends. I can't help it if you won't go with me. So don't you dare try to make me feel guilty."

Hogan wanted to go with her, and he enjoyed the whiskey all too well. But he had already been out too many times on weekdays. The boss man said if Hogan messed up one more time, he would be fired. If he lost his job, he couldn't give Gloria any money. That would make him a bad husband.

Held by his vows, he had to let her go as she pleased. For in his heart, he only wanted to make her happy, a chore that became more and more tedious.

Day after day, Hogan trudged through the disappointments of his marriage. For him, there was no turning back. Marriage was forever. The idea of a couple breaking up was inconceivable; divorce was as foreign a word as escargot.

*****

The story of Gloria Foster marrying a poor, dumb Kentucky boy amazed the locals. They figured she would wind up dead, either from booze or at the hands of an angry lover. No one was more surprised or angry than Duck. She was just supposed to keep Hogan drunk all weekend so he would mess up at work. He wanted the boss to see that his favorite boy wasn't so great after all.

Duck stewed over this blatant betrayal. He was the one who kept Gloria from killing herself all those years ago. He found her in the alleyway, drunk, alone, and about to cut her wrist with the jagged edges of the empty bottle she had just broken. He remembered looking at her sullen, mascara-smudged eyes and thinking how he couldn't let her go out that way. A beautiful woman like this should be having fun, not letting the opinions of snooty, so-called Christians bring her to the point of suicide. So he stopped her, took her to his home to sleep it off, and stayed with her until she came around to his way of thinking.

Duck and Gloria lived together for several months. They partied every evening and enjoyed each other every night until Gloria became strong enough to balk at her savior's controlling ways. They wound up fighting so much that Gloria moved into the shanty and started making money any way she could. She still partied with Duck and their friends. She just didn't want to be his puppet. No, it had to be better this way.

Duck, on the other hand, still thought of Gloria as his. The idea of Hogan being with her infuriated him. He would never let this mountain boy get the upper hand. His day would come. Everyone would see.

*****

A mid-January day brought a blustery snow. The wind and stinging flakes made Hogan pull his jacket tight, steadying himself while walking toward the car where Daddy waited to take him home after work. Hogan was glad to see him but not surprised. Daddy often showed up to give him a ride in inclement weather.

Pulling up to the curb beside Hogan's little house, neither thought anything unusual about the vacant appearance, no lights shining in the windows, no smoke from the chimney. Not happy about the fact that Gloria was out on such a bad night, Hogan tried not to let his worry show.

After saying goodbye to Daddy, he set out to get a load of firewood. He wanted to make the house nice and warm when she did come home.

Slipping through the backdoor, Hogan balanced a stack of wood in his right arm while fumbling with his left hand to find a light switch. He made his way from the kitchen to the wood stove in the living room, where he set down the load.

As he stood to look around, his eyes met with a sight that shocked his entire system. Except for a few scattered boxes and a Sears Roebuck Catalogue, the room stood completely empty.

"Where did she take our things?" he muttered to himself, wandering around the room in a desperate search for something that might make sense. Moving awkwardly about, he entered the tiny bedroom, which held nothing but a heap of his own clothes in the middle of the floor.

"Could she have found another house for us? I hope she won't need any more money."

The thought was entirely possible to Hogan. Gloria constantly bought things and did things without telling him first. Every piece of furniture she brought home while he was at work, new clothes, a refrigerator, curtains, whatever she wanted seemed to just appear.

He always felt good to think he provided her with nice things. What Hogan did not know was how she purchased nearly everything on credit in his name. Accounts at the local furniture store and dress shop remained past due. When the owners paid a visit to Gloria that afternoon demanding payment, she knew they would eventually contact Hogan.

Time was up. She had used this hillbilly for all he was worth. Besides, it wasn't fun anymore. She hated feeling beholden to him, hated how nice he was. Even his naivety, which allowed her scheming, held no interest. And she absolutely despised his goody-goody family. As far as Gloria was concerned, Hogan should go back to them and forget about her.

Not knowing her plan, Hogan sat on the floor, thumbing through pages of the Sears Roebuck Catalog as he waited for his wife. Frayed edges marked favorite sections of household goods. Ordering from the book was one thing she taught him and one small thing they each enjoyed. So she showed him the fun of picking out pictures and having that very thing show up a few days later.

On page 53, he saw the clock she ordered just after they moved in. A few more pages showcased the dishes now gone from the cupboard. Then he flipped through the women's clothing. And there, he met with the most beautiful familiar eyes. Modeling a red chiffon dress trimmed in velvet, a photo of Aunt Lilly stared back at him.

Hogan gasped for a second, but then he couldn't help but grin. He looked the picture and the woman's image over carefully to make certain it was really her. It had to be. Here was the same long, black hair; the same deep, blue eyes; the same lean figure. And if that weren't enough, she still had the same red fingernails and lips that Hogan remembered from the day she left.

"It looks like she found that place where people smile all the time," Hogan stated aloud, admiring how happy she looked.

The more he stared at the page, the more he thought he could actually see the hem of her dress billow back and forth, her head tossing back in a wide, carefree giggle.

"How about that," he giggled to himself. "Aunt Lilly ran off to California and wound up in my house."

Hogan couldn't wait to tell Mommy how he'd seen her. He imagined she would tell them all how Aunt Lilly had really lost her way by dressing in those bright clothes and acting like such a showoff. But he knew that deep down, she would really be glad to see the sight of her.

Somewhere in the middle of his thoughts, he remembered why he had been looking at the catalog in the first place.

"Where could she be?" he wondered of Gloria after realizing how late it must be.

He could sit and stew no longer. Rising from the floor, he closed the damper on the woodstove, bundled up, and headed out in search of his wife.

The best place to start, he reasoned, was at Duck's house. Pulled along by determination, he passed the alleyway where they first met. A crosswind whirled out of the now empty space, made Hogan shiver.

He heard the noise of a party in the distance. It was coming from Duck's house. Feeling certain to find Gloria, Hogan hurried toward the house. He pounded loudly on the door to make sure someone would hear. Duck opened the door laughing, a woman on his arm and a bottle of booze in his hand.

"I've come to get Gloria," Hogan informed his adversary.

Duck only laughed harder. "Have you? Well, sorry to disappoint you, friend. But she ain't here. I will tell you a little secret, though," Duck offered suspiciously.

Hogan waited with great hope to hear any information.

With a drunken swagger, Duck leaned slightly out of the doorway. "She's gone," he stated with wide eyes, waving his arms around like a magician performing a disappearing act.

"That's right, boy. She left you. She finally got tired of your pathetic, hillbilly ways. You'll never see her again."

"It's not true, "Hogan argued. "Tell me where she is. She's my wife."

"Not anymore, you idiot. Don't you get it? She never wanted you. She just wanted to spend what little money you had. Now go on back to mama's or something. You're putting a wet blanket on our party."

For the first time in Hogan's life, he wanted to hurt someone. He felt his fists clench as anger welled up in his throat. The feeling scared him so bad that he quickly turned away and retreated back into the street before he could unleash the fury that raged within.

"That's right, boy! Runaway!" Duck hollered after him. "That's all you'll ever be good at!"

A flurry of thoughts ran through Hogan's mind as he ran all the way back home. It really was true. The house was still bare. Gloria was still gone. The big, strong mountain man cried like a baby as he stoked the remaining embers in the woodstove. Curling up on the floor in front of the fire, he struggled with the pain in his heart, thinking that he would never feel warm again.

*****

The next morning found Hogan at the doorway of home. Cold, hungry, and completely devastated, he turned the knob to find Mommy wringing clothes at her washing machine. One look at the shattered expression on her son's face said it all. Feeling his pain, she threw her arms around his neck.

"Come in, come in," she told him with such compassion. "Tell me, what's the matter."

Hogan sat at the kitchen table, spilling the news of Gloria leaving amid spurts of tears.

Hearing the commotion, Allie and Pearlie Sue emerged to give support to their big brother.

"It's okay," Pearlie Sue assured. "Just come back and live with us. We love you."

Her words did make Hogan feel better. And the smell of Mommy frying bacon and eggs reminded him how hungry he was.

Allie's protective nature made her want to find this horrible woman and teach her a lesson. But Mommy would never allow it. Anyway, now that she was gone, maybe Hogan would quit all the drinking and find a nice woman to marry.

For a few days, Hogan did stay with his family. Mommy fed him well and talked to him about living right. They watched the television preacher together. She tried telling him that he was not to blame for what happened.

"Some people in this world are just evil," she told him. "What she done to you was pure evil. God won't hold it against you for getting a divorce."

Daddy asked Hogan to come work with him building houses, hoping he might be able to keep a better eye on his son that way.

But Hogan still held it all against himself. He thought and thought about the bad things he had done. Making Gloria his wife was supposed to make up for having relations with her out of wedlock. He reasoned to himself that he hadn't tried hard enough. If he couldn't be a good husband, how could he be a good son, or a good person for that matter? Surely, this punishment he felt was just. He would have to suffer through and find a way back to being good.

*****

On a Sunday morning, Hogan woke well before daybreak. Carrying a grocery bag packed with clothes, he crept through the house.

In the living room, he passed by the television. He imagined the preacher wearing a dark suit, flashing a sincere smile and spouting the words that led him to his decision on this Sunday morning.

Over and over in his head, he heard the preacher man say, "Just when you think you have nothing, that is the time to pick yourself up and take those first steps toward finding redemption. Because the moment you take redemption into your heart, all your sins will be forgiven, my friends. Only then can you know God and his everlasting peace."

Hogan wished he knew exactly where to go to find this redemption. All he knew was that he had to try, and he had to do it on his own. He couldn't stand making things worse for his family any longer.

Quiet as a mouse, he tiptoed through the kitchen. A plate of gingerbread from last night's supper sat next to the stove. Thoughts of the sweet, pungent flavor made his mouth water. Carefully, he slipped as many pieces as he could fit into a dishtowel, tied up the ends, and added the sample of home to his bag.

After one last soulful look around, Hogan drew up the courage to push open the back door. He stepped out into the cold, knowing he was on his own and yet not knowing. The only security he ever knew in his whole life faded further away with each step.

Drudging over snow-covered sidewalks, Hogan's breathe fogged ahead of him, causing a tinkling sound to echo through icy limbs, which drooped just above his head. Soon he noticed the bus station. A frosty twinkle flashed in his eyes as he figured how the bus should be able to take him straight to the place where redemption could be found. Excited, but still sad to be leaving his family, Hogan hurried to the ticket counter and stared hopefully at the destination board.

The lady behind the counter noticed his puzzled look and makeshift luggage. Convinced he was another deadbeat looking to bum a ride, she decided to hurry him along.

"Where do you want to go, Handsome? And do you have any money? Cause you can't get on the bus without buying a ticket."

"Ma'am, I need to go where I can find redemption. Can you tell me the best place to start looking?"

"Redemption? Are you some kind of nut? I'm telling you, if you don't have any money, you might as well go on."

Hogan reached in his pocket and handed the surprised clerk a five-dollar bill.

"The preacher says I need to find redemption so my sins can be forgiven. Please..." he begged, pushing the money into her hand.

"I'm afraid I don't know that much about religion," the lady apologized, still trying to figure out if this giant, childlike man in front of her really was a nut. "But I do know that five bucks will take you as far as Richmond, Virginia."

Richmond. Hogan said it in his mind, remembering a day back at Leatherwood School when the teacher pointed to it on a huge map spread out across the blackboard. Even then, he felt strangely drawn to the name, wondering about it for days. What did it look like? Were there mountains? Were the people nice?

This must be it. God must be leading him to Richmond and the redemption he needed so desperately.

Hogan cheerfully handed his ticket to the bus driver. He could see day breaking a silent brilliance across the sky as he looked through the windshield ahead. After a moment, he selected a seat near the back, placing the paper bag beneath his feet. A rumbling in his stomach seemed to match that of the bus engine as it roared off toward the sunrise.

"Don't worry, Mommy," he said to himself, thinking of her while enjoying a gingerbread cake. "I'll be back...soon as I can be forgiven and make you proud."

*****

Lottie's every muscle ached. Swollen eyes and frazzled nerves signaled an obviously broken heart. A week came and went without any word of Hogan. Lottie struggled daily with the thought of never finding him.

Nathan searched every part of Austin, as well as neighboring towns, to no avail. His son had simply vanished. Though he desperately wanted to bring Hogan back safe, his primary motivation lay in easing his wife's pain.

At home, the girls worked hard at comforting their mother. They hated to see her in such a frail state, walking around the house as if lost, wringing work-worn hands in between fits of hard sobbing.

The old pendulum clock made by Nathan's great grandfather ticked away each second. The monotonous sound mixed in Lottie's mind with her husband's words, reminding her that Hogan was a grown man who should be able to take care of himself.

But Lottie knew her son better than anyone. She knew his attributes as a loving, giving human being who trusted to the point of welcoming trouble. She also knew his determined nature; how he tried with everything inside to be independent. Unfortunately, the combination, coupled with Hogan's inability to reason, carved a rocky path. Lottie kept all this to her uneasy heart with a prayer that the worst would not be his fate.

*****

"Hey, Buddy! You gotta get up from here!"

Hogan's eyes squinted open from sleep, and a bright stream of first daylight in his face. Attempting to remember where he was, he turned toward the gruff-sounding voice.

"That's right, Sleeping Beauty," came the voice again. "Time to move along. We can't have the likes of you cluttering up the sidewalks."

Towering above like a king to a knave, the Richmond Police Officer took no pity as he goaded the poor, homeless man from the warmth of the city's heating vent.

Hogan peered up at the angry man, who was dressed neatly in a dark blue uniform with silver buttons and shiny black shoes. Struggling to get to his feet, he felt hard prodding from the officer's wooden club on his backside.

Finally making his way down the street, under the watchful eye of the law, Hogan's stomach began to rumble with hunger pains. Maybe the man at the diner on the corner would let him wash dishes again in exchange for a meal.

A month after stepping off the bus in Richmond, Hogan found himself in dire straits. A continuous battle for survival replaced his search for the one thing that brought him there in the first place.

His first evening in the big city saw him down a wide street. It beckoned with bright lights and flashing signs. Fascinated, Hogan wandered along the sidewalk until he noticed a sign that said bar, with a lit-up picture of a whiskey bottle. He hadn't had a drink since before Gloria left. Feeling overwhelmed by all the noise and crowd of people, he decided that a couple of swallows would be good. In the morning, he would start looking for redemption. The sooner he found it, the sooner he could go home.

*****

Hogan pushed open the door of "The Lucky Lady," stepped inside, and sat down at the bar. He pulled a dollar bill out of his pocket, laying it cautiously on the counter.

"Whiskey, please," he requested of the bartender, who immediately poured a glass, sat it down hard in front of his new patron, and scooped up the bill in one fluid motion.

Soon, a couple of drinks turned into a couple more. Hogan began to feel good again, more relaxed and happier than he had in weeks. A crowd gathered around the newcomer who was so friendly and generous to buy a drink.

The next thing he knew, a pretty blond-haired woman in a tight dress had worked her way through the sea of drinking buddies. She reminded him so much of Gloria that he did not attempt to resist.

She laughed with him and complimented his strong muscles. She also encouraged him not to buy any more drinks.

 "Don't spend all your money on these guys," she insisted sweetly. "Where did you come from, anyway? I haven't seen you here before."

"Indiana," Hogan answered, fully expecting that again, this painted-up woman was truly interested in him as a person.

"I've come to get a job. So I can show my family that I'm a man and can take care of myself."

The woman knew instantly that her handsome, new acquaintance was as slow and naïve as they come.

"Ah, a job. Well, you'll be needing a place to stay tonight. You know. So you'll be rested up in the morning."

Just like Gloria, she took him home with her to enjoy a night of lovemaking. In the morning, she left him sleeping in her bed. She took the rest of his money and figured he would be long gone by the time she returned.

But Hogan did not leave. Once again, he believed that physical love and true love were the same. He expected she would help him find his way, not help herself to the only money he had in the world. It never even occurred to him to check his pockets.

Hungry, he helped himself to some crackers and peanut butter that he found in one of the kitchen cabinets. Patiently, he waited in her apartment all day.

"You must be a bigger idiot than I thought!" the woman screamed at him when she returned home. "Don't you get it? I just wanted you last night. I don't want you to live with me! Now beat it! Get out of here and don't come back! You do understand that don't you?"

Throwing his coat at him, she pushed her bewildered houseguest out into the hallway, slamming the door in his face.

*****

Hogan didn't get it. Shocked and confused, he struggled to imagine how there could be more than one woman in the world who would act like she loved him one minute and be so cruel the next.

From that moment on, he figured he would have to do this all by himself. Surely there was a job out there somewhere and a place to live. But without any money, there was no place to clean up, nowhere to eat except garbage cans, nowhere to sleep except the sidewalk.

Business after business turned him away for work. All they saw was a dirty bum. People passing on the streets cringed at the smell of booze and month-old body odor.

Sometimes at night, he would sit on a park bench on the outskirts of town, cradling a nearly empty whiskey bottle gleaned from the trash. Taking the last sips, he stared up at the stars, imagining he was back home. He pretended his belly was full of shucky beans and gingerbread while longing for the warm touch of Mommy's hug, the soothing sound of Daddy's patient voice, and the fun giggles of his sisters.

He felt so far away from everything. Where was God? Why had he made this redemption so hard to find? Still, there was no turning back. There was no money for a bus. He couldn't walk home. He had no idea what direction to take. Besides, he wouldn't see his family like this. He felt as lost and ashamed as the day he left.

*****

Sam at the diner was the only person in that huge city to give Hogan even a thought of compassion. The kind-hearted cook first got a glimpse of his pitiful friend while taking the garbage out at the back of the restaurant.

Startled by the sight of a huge, dirty, shaggy-haired man crouched down in the alley, he watched in indignant horror as the beast hungrily finished a sandwich from the dumpster. Sam's initial reaction was to call the cops. Although he'd seen this many times before, it always took him by surprise.

Then he caught a look in the vagrant's eyes. Sorrow, bitter as the cold night air, seeped from behind cobalt blue spheres. The pain they cast reached into Sam's heart. He could do nothing but gaze back into them.

What was the man's story? His dark skin and black curly hair, badly in need of a trim, resembled that of a Negro. But those eyes and other facial features were something entirely different. Sam recalled childhood stories of a strange people who lived deep in the mountains along the Kentucky-Virginia border. Dubbed a "Free Race of Color" because they weren't African slaves and they weren't white, these people were shunned by the town folk. Stories were told of how they inter-married and fought on the side of the Cherokee Indians against the first British Settlers.

Marked the same as savages, the story goes that this indistinguishable race of people ventured out of the wilderness only at night to trade masterful pieces of wood and stonework in exchange for goods. Yet, they were more known for their craftiness in running moonshine stills that no revenuer would dare hunt.

One such family Sam remembered was called the Black Nobles. He and the other children were taught to be afraid of the "crazy, ill-bred lot." "You better behave, or the Melungeons will take you away and have you for their supper," came the popular disciplinary warning.

Could this man, crouched down like a scared, stray animal, be one of the Melungeons? He didn't think any of them still existed.

A few minutes of understanding passed between the pair. Sam moved toward Hogan cautiously.

"Why don't you come in and let me fix you a real sandwich," Sam offered, gesturing toward the diner's backdoor.

Hogan stood and wiped his mouth on a dirty sleeve, moving just as cautiously toward the tiny, gray-haired man wearing a long, white apron. Finally, acknowledging Sam's generosity, he replied, "No, Sir, I can't. I ain't got no money."

Scratching his head, Sam pondered a moment. This poor wretch would rather eat garbage he found on his own than take a handout.

"It's okay. I need someone to wash some dishes for me, anyway," Sam lied. "I'll pay you with a good meal. Can you wash dishes?"

"Yes, Sir," Hogan agreed, feeling a moment of good luck.

Sam led the misfit into the back washroom. It had a shower, a toilet, and a washing machine. Adjoining the washroom was another small room with a bed, a chair, and a dresser that held a small television set.

"This is where I live," Sam announced. "The owner lets me stay here as part of my pay. It ain't much. But at least I'm never late for work." He chuckled at his own humor while wiping his hands on the apron.

"I'm Sam. Do you have a name, Big Fella?"

"Hogan, John Hogan Watts."

"Well, Hogan, you're gonna have to clean up before I can let you wash dishes. Just throw your clothes in the washer there and take a shower. I have a bag of clothes here somewhere that I think will fit you. Somebody threw them out by the dumpster a couple weeks back. I don't know why I thought to save them. It just seemed like such a waste to throw away perfectly good clothes. I guess I was right."

After a bit of a pause, Sam continued, "Well, I'd better go check and see if I have orders. I'll check on you shortly."

Sam disappeared through the doorway as Hogan began to strip off layers of filthy, worn clothing. He stepped to the shower doorway. He had never been in one before. He didn't know exactly how it worked. But he liked the idea of taking a bath standing up. He worked with the knobs until hot water sprayed out all over his body. It felt so good he wished he could stay in the shower longer. But he needed to hurry and wash dishes for his new friend.

When Sam returned, Hogan had just finished dressing into a pair of cotton work pants and a flannel shirt from the bag of clothes. They fit well, and Sam could hardly believe this homeless man was in such good shape for someone living on the streets.

"OKAY, my friend," Sam said, "The kitchen is this way."

Hogan followed in silence, head down, shoulders drooped.

In the kitchen, Hogan could hear laughing and talking from customers out front. He was glad to be alone in the back. The pressure of dealing with people had become too much for Hogan. Just like Mommy, he felt anxious in a crowd, not knowing what they might think or say. Only while drinking could he enjoy the company of others.

Hogan stood at the big stainless steel sink for an hour. He tried hard to do just as Sam instructed; make sure the water is as hot as he could stand, wash the glasses first, then the plates and silverware, then the pots and pans.

After a while, the noise in the restaurant quieted to silence. Sam pushed through the double doors, pulled the apron off, and hung it on the wall.

"Finally closing time," he announced as he walked over to inspect Hogan's work. "All done?"

Hogan nodded, feeling satisfied that he had done a good job.

"Great!" Sam told him. "Then I guess I promised you a meal."

As Hogan feasted on his very first cheeseburger and fries, Sam explained how he wouldn't be able to let him stay. It ate at his conscience that this good-hearted person had no place to live.

"I'm really sorry," Sam apologized. "But I know the boss won't hire you. He'd probably put me out on the street if he knew what I've done already."

It's okay," Hogan said, attempting to reassure his kindness. "It's not so bad."

*****

For the next two weeks, Hogan continued to pass through the alleyway behind Sam's diner. More often than not, he would find his friend looking out the door for him with a paper plate of food or a paper bag with a sandwich, whatever he could put together.

One morning, Sam decided he should help his friend with more than an occasional leftover meal. This time he met Hogan with a box filled with fried chicken wings, a couple of biscuits, and a slice of apple pie.

"Hogan, I've been thinking," he said, a bit unsure of how to begin. "You've got to get out of this city, or you'll never make it. I don't know where you came from, but I can tell this just ain't the place for you either. Besides, I don't know how much longer I can keep on sneaking you food."

Hogan didn't quite understand. Sam wasn't mad or yelling at him to leave like the others. Still, he was telling him to go.

"Look, my friend. There is a little town about 40 miles east of here. It's called Farmville. It's quiet and peaceful there, and the people are much friendlier. Whatever it is you're looking for, you'll probably find it there."

Sam handed Hogan the box, then reached down to pick up a duffle bag.

"Here are the rest of those clothes I kept. And your old ones are in there too, all washed."

Still a little unsure but grateful for the help, Hogan took his friend's gifts.

"And one more thing." Sam dug his hand into his front pocket, pulling out some money folded up neatly in a clip. "This should be enough for the bus ride and maybe a meal or two until you find work or something."

"No," said Hogan backing away. "I didn't work for it."

"Listen here, Hogan. I work in this diner all day. I see all kinds of people. Some are dressed real fancy. Some are just regular hardworking folks. But I've never met anyone who drew me in like you did. There's something special about you. I don't know what it is. I just feel like I'm supposed to help you. Now take this money. Let me do what I'm supposed to do."

Sam's words were true. They made Hogan feel as though it were his duty to take the money. Slowly, he extended his left hand as Sam deposited the bills into it. With his right hand, he extended a handshake, his head and shoulders still stooped in uncertainty.

"Thank you, Sam," were the only words he could muster.

"All right. So get going. There's a bus stop one block over. Promise me you'll be on it."

Hogan nodded in obedience.

"And Hogan," Sam said with a pleading in his voice. "Promise me you'll lay off the booze too. It'll only keep you in trouble."

"I will. I promise," Hogan assured his friend while walking away, thinking maybe Sam had somehow heard the same preacher and that maybe he knew that redemption was just another bus ride away.

*****

Sam was right about Farmville. It was a lot smaller than Richmond, not as small as Austin, still Hogan felt much more at ease right away. And, on his first day in town, a small stroke of luck finally crossed his path.

While passing by the grocery store at the corner of Main Street, Hogan noticed two young guys struggling to carry crates of canned goods. As if by instinct, he tossed the duffle bag Sam gave him on top of the stack and slid his arms underneath. With a bit of a groan, Hogan took the full weight, walked the load of cans through the doors, and gently laid them just inside.

"What's going on here? Who's this?"

A short, stocky man with a full beard on his chin and a full belly over his belt questioned his employees.

"This guy must've seen we were about to drop the crates, Mr. Buckley," answered one.

"Yeah. He came out of nowhere and helped us," finished the other.

"Is that so?" Mr. Buckley asked again, eying Hogan up and down. "That just leaves two things. Who are you, and where did you come from?"

"My name's John Hogan Watts. I came from Richmond."

"Well, now. You don't look like a city fella to me," the storekeeper quizzed. "Where were you raised?"

Hogan recognized the skeptical tone. It reminded him of his first day at the cannery.

"Kentucky, Sir. Lost Creek."

"Kentucky? Lord, Son. What are you doing on this side of the Smokies?"

Hogan shrugged and kept his head down. "I need a job."

"Is that so? Well, it just so happens that I could use a good, strong hand around here to bring in crates, stock shelves, and such. You're not runnin' from the law or anything, are you?"

"No, Sir," Hogan answered emphatically.

"Good. Can you start work in the morning?"

"Yes, Sir."

"Then there's just one more thing. You'll have to get a haircut and shave. I can't have a shaggy worker running around my store."

Mr. Buckley pulled a small change purse from his pocket, opened it, and retrieved a fifty-cent piece. Handing the coin to Hogan, he continued, "Take this to Ned at the barbershop across the street. Tell him to give you a close cut, then bring my change back with you in the morning."

"Yes, Sir. Thank you. I'll be here." Hogan stated with delight in his eyes. He squeezed the coin tight and thanked Sam as well.

*****

Glancing down at the crate of canned goods, Hogan noticed the familiar label. They were green beans packed at Morgan's Cannery. The sight made him think of Mommy, and he hoped it wouldn't be long now before he could go home to see her and the rest of his family.

For the first time since Gloria left, he felt better about himself, free, and much more at ease. Stocking shelves came fairly easy. Everything was always in the same place, and the pace wasn't nearly as hurried as at the cannery.

Because Hogan had returned the next day with his change, Mr. Buckley knew he had an honest worker and took to him right away. Realizing that Hogan couldn't afford a place to live, he offered the small guesthouse next to his in town. The Buckley's wanted to rent it, but it needed a lot of work. They told Hogan he could live there as long as he fixed it up for them.

Hogan liked Mrs. Buckley. She was a tiny, stout woman, the same as her husband. Her name was Martha, but everyone called her Miss Marty. As bright and cheery as a rainbow, she always entered the store amid genuine smiles and hello's from workers and customers alike.

Miss Marty also took a liking to Hogan. She knew in her heart he held a sad story and wondered about his family if there was any.

One Friday at lunchtime, the lady of pure generosity strolled in, took position behind the deli counter, and prepared sandwiches for the entire crew.

Hogan brought up the end of the line, and Miss Marty was glad for the opportunity to strike up a conversation.

"Do you like the bologna, dear?" She asked.

"Yes'm. It's good," He answered with a bite in his mouth.

"What was your favorite sandwich as a boy?" She asked, further leading her way to solving the stranger's mystery.

Hogan thought hard about the question. "We didn't eat sandwiches," he finally admitted.

"Really? Luther says you grew up in Kentucky. Is your family still there?"

Swallowing hard to keep from choking, Hogan only shook his head in a sad response.

"I don't mean to pry, dear," Miss Marty began, sensing his reluctance.

"But I want you to know that Mr. Buckley and I are your friends. It's a real shame for anyone to be so far away from their family. We'll help you any way we can if you'll let us. Do you understand?"

Hogan responded again with a nod and a tear forming in his eye.

"I left them in Austin, Indiana," he began softly. "I wasn't a good boy. I had to go away to find redemption so I could be better and not make them ashamed anymore."

Hogan broke down and cried on Miss Marty's shoulder. The release felt so good that he opened up completely, spilling all the sorted details to Miss Marty's listening ears.

"There, there," she repeated, patting him on the back and telling him it would be all right. "You don't seem like such a bad boy to me. We all make mistakes, you know. But, you seem to really care, and that makes a right fine person in my book."

Hogan sat up and took in the kind words.

"You have to let them know you're okay," she continued. "I'm a mama myself, you know. I'd be at my wit's end if I didn't know where my son was. Just give them a call. You can use the office phone."

"I – I can't," Hogan stuttered in a confused state.

"Why not?"

"They don't have a phone."

"Oh. Well, write a letter. I'll help you. What's the address?"

Again, Hogan didn't know the information. Miss Marty knew what a slow thinker her husband's newest employee was. But it wasn't until that moment that she realized the depth of his mental deficiency. It was like nothing she had ever encountered. Here was a young man who could memorize the exact location of every can in the store. Yet, he didn't even know his parents' address.

More determined than ever, Miss Marty swore to Hogan that she would find them and let them know he was okay

That suited Hogan just fine. He really didn't want Mommy to worry. He just wanted to make her proud.

True to her word, Miss Marty began her search that afternoon. The shopkeeper's wife called the operator in Austin, Indiana. To her surprise, there was a number for Nathan Watts. The operator rang it for her and when a young girl's voice answered, she almost couldn't speak.

Lottie nearly fainted at the news.

Overjoyed, she cried and talked for more than a half-hour to the wonderful stranger on the other end.

Miss Marty assured her that she would look after Hogan and see to it that he called regularly. She explained how he believed he had shamed them and didn't know how else to make it right.

"He has a strong nature that way," Lottie told her. "We have to let him decide when the time is right."

When Hogan did eventually call, he shunned the idea of coming home.

"Not yet," he pleaded. "I'm not ready. I'm doing okay now. I just need to be a little better."

*****

Over the next several months, the Buckley's grew to think of Hogan as a member of their family. Their own son lived up north in Ohio with his wife and children. It seemed only natural to lavish their affections on the sweet, young man who had come to work at their store and live in their guesthouse.

Mr. Buckley helped Hogan fix up the two-room house on the weekends. Together they patched the leaking roof, repaired the plumbing, and gave it a coat of paint inside and out. Most evenings, Hogan would join the couple for dinner in the main house.

One evening, as Hogan was about to say goodnight, he noticed the Sears Roebuck Catalogue on the telephone table by the door. In a trance, he reached out, running his fingers over the beautiful picture on the cover.

"Would you like to take it with you?" Miss Marty asked, fascinated by his interest. When he didn't answer, she tried again, picking up the book and handing it to him. "Here, look through it as long as you like. I'll help you order something if you like."

Hogan clutched the catalog to his breast, remembering Gloria but not wanting to remember. He smiled a bittersweet smile before easing out the door. Back at his place, he scoured over each page. Oddly, this simple practice gave him a feeling of control. All he had to do was tell the clerk at the store what he wanted, and in a few days, it would be his.

At first, he began ordering a piece of clothing each week. Since he only had the few clothes that Sam gave him the night he left Richmond. Miss Marty encouraged him to arrange his ordering that way as a sort of allowance from each week's pay.

Soon, he received his own catalog at the post office. It was his first sign of independence. He couldn't wait to make his next order on the form with his own name typed neatly at the top.

Without thinking, he splurged on ordering an entire outfit, including leather work boots. After paying for his purchase, he came up short on paying his electric bill. Mr. Buckley patiently counseled him on spending habits and the evils of buying what we can't afford. Hogan insisted that he understood and he would be more careful. Still, the catalog was like a drug to him. Shopping in a store didn't have that same effect. Something about dreaming over all the items at his leisure and the ease in which they came gave Hogan the same confidence as drinking.

*****

"Hey, Hogan! Come here a minute."

Hogan looked up from where he was stacking crates out back of the store after closing. Joe and Lewis sat in their car, waving for him to come over.

"We've got a favor to ask," began Joe, as Hogan approached the driver's side window. "You've been a good buddy ever since you saved us with those crates that day. We thought you might help us out again."

Pleased to be asked for help, Hogan felt inclined to do whatever his friends asked.

"See, we have these dates tonight," Lewis chimed in, "And we want to have something special for them. Only, the guy at the store won't let us buy it. He says we're just kids,"

"Have you ever heard of strawberry wine?" Joe asked in a spurt.

Shaking his head, Hogan was a little confused.

"It's a drink. Girls really like it. But since we can't buy it, we thought you might ride with us to the store and buy it for us. We'll give you the money."

"Yeah," Lewis insisted. "Can you help us out?"

Well aware of Hogan's slow nature, the youngsters were confident they could persuade him into going along and that he wouldn't realize he had done anything wrong.

"Okay," Hogan agreed, climbing in the back seat, as Joe and Lewis handed him congratulatory pats on the back.

The liquor store was several miles out of town on a dirt road. Lights glowed around the building, beckoning those with a thirst.

Hogan instantly recognized the familiar signs. There wasn't a bottle of liquor to be found in Farmville. All these months, it had been easy for Hogan to keep his promise to Sam. Now, it was right in front of him. Thoughts of the taste and delicious numbing sensation caused his mouth to water.

For a moment, he wondered if he was doing wrong by these boys. Still, Strawberry wine sounded innocent enough. He reckoned that would be all right.

Once inside, the temptation was too great. He came back out to the car with a jug of wine under one arm and a bottle of whiskey under the other.

"Way to go, Hogan!" Joe said loudly.

"You're the best!" Lewis proclaimed.

The boys dropped Hogan off at his house and drove away, leaving him with mixed emotions. It made him happy to please his young friends, but he struggled with his own weakness at wanting a drink so badly.

Sitting in his living-room chair, he caressed the bottle, admiring the caramel color and how the dim light cast a prism of brightness through it. He carefully broke the seal of the cap and raised the bottle to his lips. The liquid burned all the way down, sending a warm sensation to each extremity.

Appeasing the conflict in his mind, he figured that just a few sips here and there wouldn't hurt anything. Besides, he was home, by himself, not in a bar or anywhere like that. No other men around to make him feel worthless. No woman to fool with his emotions.

Yet, the bottle won out, sip after longer sip, until it was all gone before the night was over.

*****

Hogan woke the next afternoon to a pounding on the door by Mr. Buckley. When he didn't come to the house for breakfast or lunch, Miss Marty became worried and sent her husband to make sure he was all right.

Blurry-headed and staggering, Hogan realized enough to know he didn't want to be found in such a state. Rather than answering the door, he went to the shower to revive his senses and brush his teeth to remove the tale-tale odor.

"Hogan! Hogan!" shouted Mr. Buckley.

Fearing something was terribly wrong, Mr. Buckley used his key to go in.

He stormed through the tiny living room to meet Hogan coming out of the bathroom.

"What's wrong, son? Are you sick?" Mr. Buckley asked, noticing the wet hair and grimacing look on Hogan's face.

"Sort of," Hogan answered in a half-lie, not wanting the man, who was like his second father, to be ashamed of him.

"Martha has been worried sick about you. I hope it's not the flu."

Hogan shrugged, "I'll be okay."

"Just the same, I'll have her bring you some soup. If it gets worse, we'll go see Doc Smith. Now get some rest. You look awful."

Hogan tried to smile in agreement, feeling even worse to have such a secret.

After that, it became a weekly routine for Joe and Lewis to take Hogan to the liquor store. Soon, his body adjusted to the effects, making it easier to hide, also making it harder to go without. Hogan didn't know the term alcoholic. He couldn't understand the disease that claimed his mind and body. He only knew that with the drink in his system, he felt more comfortable and in control. Why would he want to give that up?

During the next few years, Hogan kept his simple routine and his shameful secret. He never missed a day at work or a meal at the Buckley's. He was careful to hide his empty bottles, throwing them out at the liquor store dumpster when he replenished his supply.

He also began calling Mommy regularly, just to hear her voice say she loved him and wanted to see him. He always finished the call by reassuring that it wouldn't be much longer. One particular conversation led to asking for money. His penchant for booze and catalog ordering more than drained his pay. He couldn't ask the Buckley's for more money. They were already too good to him. Besides, Mr. Buckley's talk about overspending made him too afraid to ask. So he explained to Mommy that he had ordered a telephone so he could call her without bothering the boss man. She was more than willing to help, another routine that grew more frequent as time passed.

*****

"This must be the infamous Hogan I've heard so much about."

"Hogan, I'd like you to meet my son, John."

Hogan abruptly set the can of corn on the shelf, turned toward the voices, and faced a stranger who held out his hand for shaking.

"John has decided to move his family back here from Ohio. Isn't that wonderful?" asked an excited Mr. Buckley. "He's going to learn the business and take over when I retire."

Hogan smiled with a hint of bitterness.

"Now, son, don't be that way. You know the Mrs. and I are getting on in years, and I need to know that someone will carry on. But don't worry. It won't be tomorrow."

John Buckley was 37-years-old. A little taller and a lot thinner than his dad, he carried himself with a pious air, from the neatly pressed three-piece suit that seemed a bit much for a grocery store, to the manner in which he looked down his nose toward a perfectly combed mustache. Hogan found it hard to imagine that he was the son of such dear people.

"Well then," Mr. Buckley began. "John and his wife, Patricia, will be staying at our house with their kids, John Jr. and Cindy. I just wanted you to know you're still welcome to come for meals, the same as always."

That was fine with Hogan. He hadn't expected anything different. It was nice for the Buckley's to have their whole family together. That night, he called mommy just to talk. He didn't even ask for any money.

Things began to change around the grocery store. Slowly at first, but all the workers began to notice how John took more and more control. Cashiers were given strict orders about dress and hairstyles. Box boys could no longer "lollygag around," and everyone had to wear matching aprons with "Buckley's" embroidered across the front.

"I don't know, Pop. He's just so slow."

"He's a fine worker. The most dependable I've had in years."

"I know he's been good to you and Mom. I'm grateful for that, but sometimes we have to think about the business end of things."

Mr. Buckley and his son strolled across the backyard as they talked, watching Hogan disappear into the guesthouse after leaving from dinner.

"Think about it, Pop," John continued.

"He doesn't pay you a thing in rent. Most of the time, you pay the majority of his utilities, and yet you pay him a full wage. This is not the way to plan for retirement."

"Son, I also understand that you have graduated college and have a good head for business. But sometimes, we have to think about the human side of things. That boy has helped us out around here. Your mother thinks the world of him. It's true he needs looking after. I'm proud we've been able to do that for his mother all these years. It's the Christian thing to do."

John thought quietly for a moment, then turned to his dad with a cocked eyebrow.

"I didn't want to have to say anything, but I'm pretty sure I smelled liquor on his breath a couple of times."

"Nonsense, John. That sounds like jealousy talking to me. Just because Hogan has been like family these past few years doesn't mean he's going to replace you as our son."

"Pop, I'm not making this up. I really don't think you should trust him so much. You said he has trouble with money. With guys like that, who knows what they might decide to take."

"Now that's enough. Hogan Watts is not a regular guy. He doesn't have a dishonest bone in his body. He doesn't think that way. Even if he does take a sip of liquor now and again, I don't hold that against him."

Mr. Buckley paced back and forth in frustration.

"Son, I'm as proud as can be that you want to take over the store when I retire. And I know you'll be doing things your way, as it should be. But I'm making one stipulation, and I'll not hear another word about it. As long as I'm alive, Hogan will always have a job here and a place to live."

* * * * *

Five more years passed with little incident. John had all but taken control of the store. Mr. Buckley and Miss Marty began taking longer vacations. His full retirement lay just around the corner.

On the spur of the moment, Hogan decided the time was right to make his own trip. He wanted to see his family and felt confident enough to face them.

Mommy's eyes gushed with tears at the news of his coming. He only promised to stay for a few days, but Mommy didn't care. She couldn't wait to see her boy, to hug his neck and see for herself that he was okay

A lot had changed for the Watts since Hogan left. Allie attended a college in Kentucky where she met a boy from Scottsburg - a neighboring town to Austin and their biggest high school rival. After dating for one year, they married and made their home on a farm in Scott County.

Pearlie Sue also met her husband at college. Several years older than his bride, he was a military man from South Carolina. He was happy to settle down in Indiana so she could be near her family.

Daddy continued to work hard at his carpentry.

Eventually, he built a brand new house just a mile down the road from Allie and her new family, so they could all live close by.

Everyone seemed to adjust well to life in southern Indiana. As more of their Kentucky family and neighbors found their way up north and the locals seemed to accept them better, life carried on peacefully. Still, they missed the absence of one beloved family member. They thrilled with excitement the day Daddy went to pick Hogan up from the bus station.

Mommy spent all day cooking an old-fashioned feast, just the way he liked. The table was spread with chicken and dumplings, new potatoes from the garden, shucky beans, and of course, gingerbread for dessert.

The family hung close together for three days, as if absorbing all the lost time.

Early summer's climate provided the perfect atmosphere. They walked through the garden each morning, explored the wood's vegetation in the afternoon, and gathered under a huge sycamore tree each evening, sharing stories and laughing while the locusts sang until dusk.

His impending departure brought more tears and questions as to why he had to go.

"Farmville is my home now," he told Mommy as she clung hard to his neck.

"I'm a man there. Miss Marty needs me around, and she looks after me too."

Mommy finally understood what her son meant; all his life, he just wanted to be in a place where he belonged; where people weren't mean, and he felt useful.

Try as she might, she hadn't been able to provide him that; such simple, basic needs. She reckoned that was all anyone really wanted. If he had found that in Virginia, she had to be happy for him.

"Maybe you'll come see me and stay at my house," Hogan invited, getting in the car to leave.

"Sure we will," Mommy promised. "Real soon, I hope."

And so, as quickly as he decided to come home, he left them again, wondering how long it might be before the next time.

*****

The next day back at work, Hogan steadily stacked packs of cigarettes on bins next to the front counter. His mind focused on matching the same color packs when he noticed her walk in.

John's wife, Patricia, came to the store every day just as Miss Marty had for over 30 years. Yet, the feeling of her entrance was very different. She always marched straight to the office without speaking to anyone and always left looking highly perturbed.

This day, her mood seemed different still. She passed closely behind Hogan, leaving the aroma of her perfume wafting around his head. He couldn't help but notice how beautiful she was. Long, wavy, auburn hair cascaded down delicate shoulders, which emphasized a tiny waist. She always wore tight skirts and blouses.

As Patricia made her way to the office, she looked back to notice Hogan peering at her legs. A wink from her big, green eyes caused Hogan to jerk his head back to the cigarettes, a blush creeping up his neck and settling on his cheeks. He always thought she would be even more beautiful if she smiled once in a while. But that look only made him uncomfortable. Working so close to the office, he couldn't help but hear the harsh sounding tone in Patricia and John's conversation. Moments later, she came back out, determination glowing from rosy cheeks.

"Well, Hogan. It's good to have you back," She told him in a sultry voice, walking even closer than before. "We've all missed you."

Determined not to look her way, Hogan kept busy with his duties. Yet, he could not ignore the feeling of her hand squeezing his bicep.

"See you around," She spoke sweetly while moving around him toward the door.

Her actions seemed so curious to Hogan. He recognized these signals from before. But Patricia was a married woman. He wouldn't allow himself to think of her that way.

But Hogan wasn't the only one to notice Patricia's signals. John watched with hate-filled eyes from behind the office window, salivating at the chance to get rid of this thorn in his side.

*****

Patricia never wanted to move back to Farmville. She enjoyed the excitement of big city life in Ohio and fought the idea vehemently when John told her of his plans. The longer they lived in the small town, the more stagnant she felt. Her blood heated with resentment at each thought of missing formal parties at the accounting firm where John worked. The trendy galas, days spent at the salon and shopping, all seemed like a distant memory, and she vowed to have it all back one day.

Determining that her only chance would be for John to sell the store, she worked on his emotions daily.

"You promised me this was temporary, but I don't see you getting any closer to telling your father what we planned," she scolded him.

"I'm trying to turn this store into something a big chain would want to buy. That takes time," he argued back.

"All I see is a spineless man who hasn't got the guts to stand up to his father. Five years I've waited for you to do something with this dump. Your father should have signed this thing over to you already, and you just sit back and say nothing. Meanwhile, our children's education is suffering in these backward schools."

"You expect me to believe you're worried about our children? They've never been happier. You're only worried about yourself, your precious image, and high-priced friends."

"What a big man you are." Undaunted, she spoke in a strong whisper, "Well, so what if I want my life back. You bet I want the best for us and our children. And yes, my good looks are wasting away here. You used to be proud to enter a room with me and watch heads turn. You used to enjoy making me happy, but I'm dying here, and you don't seem to care in the slightest. Well, I can still make a few heads turn, even in this hick town."

She scooped her purse up from the desk and turned to leave.

"Just what do you mean by that?" he questioned, following her to the door.

"Just do what you do best, Mr. coward. Stand there and watch." With that, she walked out, closed the office door, and approached Hogan with her evil intentions.

*****

After that day, John's resentment of Hogan turned to a cold, calculating hatred. He delighted in ordering him to perform all the tasks no one else wanted; scrubbing the employee bathrooms, disposing of rotten meat, and soured dairy products.

All the while, John hoped his enemy would get disgusted enough to quit. Since his dad would never allow him to fire Hogan, he believed the next best thing would be if he left on his own.

At the same time, Patricia continued playing her cruel games. Like a hungry cat, she toyed with her prey, flashing green eyes and digging her claws in deeper.

Neither of the pair realized how deep Hogan's loyalty ran toward the elder Buckley's. He still worked as though it were all for Mr.

Buckley and came to dinner to visit with Miss Marty. None of the childish antics carried out by John and Patricia phased him, at least not outwardly.

Indeed, John was extremely jealous of his father's interest in Hogan. He didn't understand how this person could walk into the picture and instantly gain the attention he craved his whole life.

As a child, his father's time was always spent at the store. During his teenage years, he worked at this store, along with other classmates. But he always felt pressured to be better than everyone.

When the chance came to return home and help his father, he secretly hoped they would finally be able to bond, and even though he promised Patricia it was only temporary, his desire was for her to settle down and enjoy small-town life.

Reality's slap in the face left John bitter. Patricia's constant needling weakened his spirit and hardened his heart.

Late one night, as Hogan busied himself hiding whiskey bottles in the trash can behind his house, he felt an odd presence nearing. He turned around nervously to find Patricia standing next to him. Her soft complexion illuminated beneath the dim glow of the porch light. Her long nightgown flowed gracefully in the gentle night air, tossing about effortlessly to reveal bare feet.

"Miss Patricia," Hogan acknowledged, attempting not to sound startled.

"Nice night, isn't it?" she responded.

"I was taking out a little trash of my own. I thought I saw you down here, so I decided to say hello, get a little fresh air, you know."

Patricia lifted the lid on the can to add a small bag of garbage when she caught a whiff of the unmistakable odor. Upon closer inspection, she noticed the top of a whiskey bottle shining from between two boxes.

"Well, well," she said accusingly as she carefully lifted the evidence from its hiding place. "John was right."

Hogan's heart beat fast from the thought of being caught. Like a child with a pocketful of unpaid candy, he didn't know whether to run or cry for mercy.

"It's all right with me," Patricia condoned, noticing Hogan's worried expression.

"In fact, if you have any more, I'll take a drink with you."

"No, ma'am," Hogan answered, looking away. The shape of her body showing through the nightgown embarrassed him.

"What's the matter Hogan?" she asked in a whisper. "Are you afraid I'm going to tell?"

With a sexy gait, the lonely, cold-hearted woman stepped closer. She flashed lustful eyes toward her companion as she looked him up and down.

Patricia's movements caused Hogan's body to quiver and his cheeks to blush. Her actions reminded him of Gloria and the woman in Richmond. Scared and nervous, he didn't know what to do.

"Why Hogan, you're shaking," she observed.

"You know, this shy little boy act from such a big, strong man is really sexy."

She reached up to stroke Hogan's face.

"Don't worry," she promised softly. "Your secret is safe with me. I don't want anything from you. I just want to drive my husband crazy until I get what I want from him. You understand, don't you?"

After speaking, Patricia backed away, keeping her eyes on Hogan for several steps. Turning toward the sidewalk, which connected the guesthouse to the main house, she blew a goodnight kiss in his direction.

Hogan stood paralyzed; the moonlit vision of Patricia in her nightgown trapped in his mind.

*****

The young Mrs. Buckley's moonlight escapade turned out to be the final straw for her husband. He returned home that night just in time to see her walking up from the guesthouse. His blood boiled at first, but sadness and a weakened spirit overtook the anger. When Patricia crept into their bedroom, he was sitting in the bedside chair; hands folded in his lap, dark, sullen eyes gaping up at her.

"Oh, you're home," she stated, removing her robe and hanging it on the back of the door. She studied his empty look of indifference. What was he thinking? Had she gone too far? Why didn't he just say something?

"OKAY, Patricia. You win. I can't fight all three of you."

John finally broke the silence with his statement of defeat.

"What are you saying? You're going to sell the store? We can go home now?" she antagonized. "And who else are you fighting besides me?"

"I'm saying that for the past five years, I've tried to make everybody happy. But I can't. So, I'm giving up. Pop knows you want me to sell the store. That's why he won't sign it over to me. Because he also knows, if we sell the store, Hogan would probably end up out of a job.

Pausing for a moment, John walked over to the window, which overlooked the walkway leading to the guesthouse.

"For the life of me, I can't understand how Dad could think more of that retarded drunk than he does his own son."

"Your dad knows you can take care of yourself. Hogan is a charity case.

I'm sure he just thinks he's doing the Christian thing," Patricia said in an almost consoling manner.

"And you?" John said with more fire.

"Don't talk to me about Christian things. You've made a fool of me all over town, flaunting and flirting with every guy you see, especially that one down there," he stated, pointing an accusing finger out the window.

"I didn't know how else to get your attention!" she spouted back." I've been miserable all this time too. You haven't cared about me. Your mission has been to get rid of Hogan. You know, a lot of women would have left you a long time ago."

"Well, I suppose none of that matters now. Like I said, I give up. We'll go back to Ohio, so you can have your life back. Dad will just have to hire another manager."

*****

It took nearly a month to hire and train someone to take over the store. Mr. Buckley finally decided on a nice, middle-aged man who had plenty of experience and also enough patience to deal with Hogan.

The elder Buckley's were sad to see their children leave, but they understood. Patricia's assumption of their confidence in John's ability was correct. On the other hand, Hogan needed looking after. Even though he came to them as a stranger, and they had never met Lottie, they felt beholden to give some comfort to another who could not be close enough to see her incapable son taken care of.

Another ten years rolled out as Hogan's routine teetered precariously on the edge of disaster. Days of menial labor turned into nights of steady drinking. Like a child, he hid the behavior that he knew was wrong. By now, he had no choice in the matter. He didn't know there was a disease called alcoholism. He just knew that if he went many days without drinking, he got sick. To keep from going through the vomiting, shaking, and sweating, he got the whiskey any way he could. If he didn't have money for a taxi, he walked the 4-mile round trip to the liquor store on the outskirts of town.

Somewhere along the line, Hogan lost sight of the redemption that took him away from home in the first place. He became complacent in his search.

Not that he had forgotten his family, he visited them a handful of times but was always in a hurry to get back to Virginia. He knew he wouldn't be able to get the drink while he was there.

He did call Mommy on a regular basis. More often than not, he called for help in paying a bill. She became so used to the asking that she set aside an amount for him each month. She could also tell how pained he sounded in asking. So she began the routine of gently asking him first how much he might need.

He didn't have the ability to reason. Yet this is what was meant by pride going before a fall. And it was this same skewed feeling of pride that told him it was better to ask for money than admit not being able to take care of himself.

*****

Fluffy, white clouds rolled along the horizon on a bright spring morning after a night of thunderstorms held the community hostage. Hogan awoke to the sound of a siren. Louder and closer came the eerie signal of death or disaster.

Looking out his kitchen window, he saw the white ambulance with orange lights flashing turn into the drive of the main house. Frozen in terror, Hogan thought about what to do. He didn't really want to know if anyone was hurt or sick. He couldn't bear to think about what it might mean. All he wanted was to live each day just like it was. It was too scary to imagine anything changing.

Then he thought about Grandma Annie and the clanging from the cast iron bell, echoing across the holler. She always knew what to do. Always so calm and unafraid, she took care of all the people back home at Lost Creek. He remembered the look and feel of her brown, leathery hands as she placed them on his cheeks to feel for fever and the seriousness in her eyes while mixing up medicines from plants and roots. She never played, and she rarely smiled. Still, her love for family was understood.

Grandma Annie passed away nearly 15-years-ago. He remembered how sad he was when Mommy told him on his first trip back to Indiana. Examining his own hands, he noticed some resemblance; the same long fingers and dark skin, so dark there was a hint of blue. Maybe he could do something to help.

Like a bullet being fired, Hogan shot out the door and charged up the sidewalk to the Buckley's house. Suddenly, he was met with an overwhelming sadness. Two men dressed in uniforms carried out a body, which was laid on a stretcher and covered with a sheet. Following behind was Mrs. Buckley, sobbing into a cloth handkerchief. Again, Hogan froze at the sight. He was too late.

"Oh Hogan, He's gone! He's gone on to heaven!" Miss Marty lamented, grabbing her friend around the neck when she noticed him standing there.

Hogan hugged her back as the two sobbed for several minutes.

"Why? How?" he finally asked.

"Oh my dear boy," she began, touched by his sincerity. "I guess it was just his time."

Miss Marty wiped her eyes and nose. Then she fidgeted with the waistband on her skirt.

"He stayed up all night watching the storm," she continued. "Oh, how he loved a good storm. He was never afraid. I always cover my head under the blanket. But Mr. Buckley, he thrilled at the brilliance of a streak of lightning."

Envisioning her husband's final moments, her face turned somber,

"I found him this morning in his chair by the window."

Two days later, spring showers returned for Mr. Buckley's funeral. It seemed as though the whole town closed down in order to say goodbye to one of Farmville's most beloved citizens.

Hogan felt obliged to keep his distance from the family, though he took the passing of his friend as hard as any of them. Besides, he still felt very uncomfortable around John and Patricia. The son and daughter-in-law stayed on with Miss Marty for two weeks, helping to set their father's final wishes in motion.

*****

As expected, the bulk of Mr. Buckley's estate went to his wife. Buckley's grocery store, however, was willed to John. True to his nature as a loving father, he realized that his son deserved whatever means the store could provide. True to his word, he made sure Hogan had a job as long as he was alive, keeping his faith that between Miss Marty and the good Lord, his slow-witted friend would find a way.

"Don't you think it's a bit soon to be talking about selling the store?"

Miss Marty walked into the sitting room as John finished a phone conversation. He turned to his mother to meet that look of disapproval capable of making a burglar back away from a jewelry store.

"Now, Ma," he said in an attempt to turn the tables. "We've been over this a dozen times. You know I don't have a choice, and I don't have a lot of time to take care of this."

"I understand that it's your choice. It just seems so sad. That store is your father's legacy. It kept a lot of people in a job for over 30 years, and it more than made us a good living."

"Yes, but privately owned grocery stores are becoming a thing of the past. They can't compete with chain supermarkets that buy in huge quantities and sell for less.

Believe me, Mom. I've looked at the books. Buckley's was on its way out, whether Dad was still alive or not. At least this way, most of the people will keep their jobs instead of shutting the doors forever."

Miss Marty knew her son's argument made sense. Still, the sentiment in her heart would not go away so easily.

"Well, choice or no choice, you won't blame me if I'm not over-joyed with your big deal, will you?"

"Of course not, Mom. You know, this isn't exactly easy for me either. But if I don't do something now, everything Dad worked for his whole life will be gone."

"So," Miss Marty concluded in guarded acceptance. "Who's this company you've been talking to?"

"Piggly Wiggly, some reps are coming out tomorrow to look at the store. If they like what they see, we'll probably have a deal by next week."

"That soon, eh? And our employees? Who decides who stays and who goes?"

"Ma, you know I can't tell them how to run their company. But I do know that Dad kept more employees than he should have. His heart was too big for his own good."

John hesitated, searching for the right words.

"You have to let go of him, too," he finally blurted out with a breath of exhausted resolution.

"What are you talking about?"

"Hogan. You can't keep holding yourself responsible for him. He needs more help than you or Dad could ever give him."

"I don't expect you to understand. In fact, I never blamed you for being a little jealous. But the fact is, having him here brought us a lot of comfort."

Miss Marty positioned herself on the couch so she could look out the window, her hands placed calmly in her lap.

"I can't really explain it. He's just a poor soul that doesn't seem to have anyone else."

"What about his own family? I know you talk to his mother. Why don't they come get him and take care of him?"

"It's not as easy as all that. Hogan may seem very simple-minded on the outside, but he has deep feelings. One of those is to feel independent. As crazy as it sounds, he feels more on his own here in our guest house with a steady job than he ever could back home under the close protection of his family."

There would never be a true understanding between mother and son on this subject, only a regrettable acceptance of the way things are.

*****

All too soon, changes engulfed the local grocery store. The weatherworn "Buckley's" sign came down. In its place, a bright, red "Piggly Wiggly" sign emblazoned the front of the building. Shiny, chrome grocery carts lined the doorway inside, as new cash registers, shelving, and modern displays seemed to appear overnight.

Once the physical transformation was complete, new management stepped in to streamline the workforce. As expected, Hogan and a handful of others were not considered to be Piggly Wiggly material. Incapable of grasping their technical stocking system, his only option was to be a bag boy. But just like Mommy, Hogan's personality could not handle the fast pace, or the demands of several people gathered around waiting for help.

Hogan's heart sank as his fate closed in. The new management would not pay him just to unload crates and take out trash. Those duties were divided among the bag boys. No way around it; he was out.

All those who were let go received generous final pay, along with an apathetic wish of "good luck."

In that instant, Hogan became lost again. It never crossed his mind that he would ever do anything else or that he would have to do anything else. He stared blankly at the check in his hand. A wrenching in his gut felt just like the night Gloria left. His body twitched with anxiety and the need for a drink.

How would he be able to live now? At 47-years-old, he still felt like a little boy trying to grow up. Everything he ever relied on was gone. Miss Marty seemed so feeble these days. He couldn't expect her to take care of him. Back home felt so far away. He never wanted to hurt Mommy. Still, something deep inside would not allow him to return.

Indiana never became home in his heart. It could never replace Kentucky hollers, where he roamed and felt so free. Instinctively, he knew he would never feel that again.

Hogan closed his eyes, picturing himself on the hillside. A fallen oak tree lay at his feet. He felt a whisper of a breeze escape from the woods to his left as he lifted the heavy axe overhead. Strength and power surged through his body while the axe cut swiftly through the air before splitting a huge gash into the log.

Breathing in that moment of a job well done, his mind took him next to a church meeting in a meadow. He stood surrounded by kinfolk and neighbors, lifting their voices louder and louder in song. The preacher's thunderous tone crashed against powerful chords of praise, which shattered across the atmosphere above. Then, in a sudden moment of silence, pieces of worship showered down to earth, covering their sins and filling their hearts with harmony for another day.

*****

"Hogan. Hogan, are you in there?"

Lightly tapping on the guesthouse door, Miss Marty called out to her friend. Not wanting to be intrusive but at the same time concerned, she continued to summon for him.

She had not seen him the whole day before. Knowing he was upset about his job and future, she let him be when he didn't show up at dinner. But after breakfast the next morning, worry took the forefront.

Miss Marty put together a plate of pancakes and sausage, smothered in warm cane syrup, one of Hogan's favorites. After covering the dish with plastic wrap, she balanced it with her left hand, steadying her steps with a cane on the right.

She hadn't made the walk down the sloping sidewalk to Hogan's in years, and she felt her knees grind with each shifting of her weight. Reaching his front door, the 70-year-old woman panted for air and the relief of seeing that Hogan was all right.

Several minutes of knocking passed with no response.

"Hogan, I know you're in there. Why won't you answer the door?"

She couldn't stand another minute, so she tried the knob. It turned freely in her hand. Continuing to balance between the plate and cane, Miss Marty eased the door open. A strong smell of booze hit her nostrils as she entered the darkness of his tiny living room.

Setting Hogan's breakfast plate on an end table, she fumbled around to open the nearest window shades. Streaks of morning sunlight shot across the room. Her eyes followed the rays over to the couch, where Hogan's body lay pale and lifeless.

"Lord no!" she cried out loud, walking her fastest to reach him. His legs dangled over the edge of the couch while the rest of his body stretched out across it. One empty whiskey bottle sat on the floor by his head, a half dozen more randomly scattered on the coffee table.

Miss Marty eased herself down next to Hogan with the help of her cane. Stroking her friend's thick, black hair, she cried and prayed.

"Please, Lord, don't take him now, not this way. He's tried so hard to be normal, to have people treat him normal. But the world is so cruel. Lord, I know you can see inside his heart. He's just a child, and no child should have to suffer as he has suffered. Please. He needs your help now more than ever. Please."

Her sobbing intensified to think of his sad demise and so soon after losing her husband. It was more than she could bear. Then she thought about Hogan's mother. How would she ever explain this to her? She has always assured Lottie that Hogan was doing well. She never believed her own son's stories of Hogan drinking. She just thought he wanted to make him look bad out of jealousy.

Guilt welled up in her throat.

"I'm so sorry, Hogan. I would've helped you. I swear I would have."

Patting his cheek one last time, she felt a burst of warm breath on her arm. He was alive.

"Hogan! Hogan!" she called to him, patting his face harder to get some response.

Feeling her prayer answered, she scrambled to her feet, found the phone, and dialed the operator for an ambulance.

"Hang on, Honey," she pleaded. "Help is on the way."

Clenching a grateful hand to her heart, she sent a silent thank you up to heaven. Perhaps this time, the sounding sirens would signal a miracle.

*****

A hummingbird flittered outside the hospital room window on the morning Hogan awoke. Back and forth, up and down, it moved about with such grace and energy, holding the excitement of a new beginning.

His sense of smell came first, as the aroma of coffee and antiseptic aroused those membranes. Slowly, he became aware that he was waking from sleep. But he did not know where or why.

This was a different sort of bed. The head portion bent upward, and there were metal rails down each side.

What was this funny nightgown thing? And who was this woman in a white dress standing beside him, holding his wrist?

Finally, his eyes focused enough to see Mommy and Daddy, Allie and Pearlie Sue standing at the foot of the bed.

"His vital signs have greatly improved," the nurse told his family. "I'll let the doctor know he's coming around."

Mommy smiled at the nurse, then rushed to her son's side. She pressed his face in her hands while kissing his forehead.

"I was so scared. I thought we had lost you," she said in a quivering voice.

Though happy to see them all, Hogan was still completely puzzled. He worked his fingers and toes and took in deep breaths. Everything felt real. But try as he might, he could not remember what he did before going to sleep. All he could see in his mind were vivid dreams.

Mommy knew her son would not understand the details of his sickness. He had been in a coma for nine days. Alcohol poisoning nearly shut down entire body systems. He was kept alive at the hospital by oxygen and fluids pumping into his veins.

The doctor told them he must have been drinking heavily for at least 20 years. He talked to them about cirrhosis of the liver, alcoholism, and treatment. Hogan could "dry out" in the hospital, he told them, and if he came out of the coma, he might have a chance. But if he ever drank again, it most likely would be his death.

"It's hard enough for someone of normal intelligence to overcome their cravings," the doctor said. "Your boy is going to need a lot more help, because he won't understand the disease or the dangers. If he survives, you may consider admitting him to a facility that is equipped to handle people with limited mental abilities."

Mommy thought about the doctor's words as she watched her son come back to life. She also thought about her uncle back home, who made moonshine for money. Several times she suspected he gave Hogan sips. Now she knew that's how he got "the taste."

Her heart ached with guilt for not being strong enough to stand up to her uncle. She recalled many times how he rode up on a mule and took young Hogan off with him against her pleadings. But that's just how it was. You didn't cross your elders, no matter how wrong they may be. And you didn't do anything to cause a family squabble, no matter what.

She would never know about the cruel guys from the cannery and Gloria using alcohol to control Hogan for her benefit or how he struggled in his heart and soul to find redemption and a way back to making them proud.

During the time Hogan had been in the coma, Allie and Pearlie Sue researched options, from government agencies to local rehab centers. One thing remained clear. Hogan would never be able to work again.

He had no money or retirement benefits. In this day and time, no one would hire a man with his type of learning disability. Yet, the sisters would not accept an institution as their brother's only choice. He worked all his life. Somehow he should qualify for a social security payment that would allow him to live on his own.

The thought of having Hogan classified as mentally disabled didn't seem exactly right either. They only saw him as too kind and too trusting. And even though he had trouble following instructions or learning book- work, he was remarkable at remembering events of the past, including exact date and time, names, what people wore, and what the weather was like.

Still, if he could receive a monthly check, they would find a house for him back in Indiana, where they could all help him. At least he would be free of mean co-workers and bosses who didn't understand. As grateful as they all were to the Buckley's, it felt like the right time to bring their brother home.

To everyone's delight, they found out that he did qualify. And they all agreed that the long process required to make it happen was nothing compared to the gain of a stable future for their loved one. Now that Hogan had regained consciousness, they couldn't wait to tell him their plans.

*****

The next day found Hogan much more lucid and responsive. He was even able to get out of bed, a bit wobbly at first, but even so, it felt like a tremendous step forward. During the doctor's visit, he told them all that Hogan was actually lucky to have been in a coma during the worst part of withdrawal.

"Now he can focus strictly on recovery," he said.

The doctor continued by attempting to speak with Hogan about his condition, what put him in the hospital and what he had to do to get well. The women took turns translating to Hogan, hoping and praying to make him understand his situation and what had to happen from here. Daddy stood by in silent approval.

"It's all gonna be fine," Mommy told Hogan, the conviction in her voice coming through more clearly than anyone had ever heard. With this confidence, she began the inevitable discussion.

"You'll like living in Indiana now. It's not like it was back then. It's much better. You'll see." She patted her son's hand and waited for some response.

"No," came the seemingly nonchalant answer, which shocked them all to silence, except for Allie.

"You haven't even thought about it," she argued, acting more than a little annoyed.

"It's okay. We just started talking," Mommy pleaded, hoping to calm her daughter's fiery and determined emotions.

"It's not okay," Allie shot back. "All these years, we've worried sick about him. First, not knowing where he was or if he was even alive. Then, not knowing if he was taking care of himself. Look at you, Mommy. You haven't really had a minute's peace since he left. You're afraid to leave the house because he might call. And you're afraid to spend any money because he might need something. I just don't see that anything will be alright unless he comes back with us, where you can see for yourself that he's taken care of and where we'll all be close enough to help."

Allie sat down on the edge of the hospital bed, looking Hogan squarely in the eyes

"You're my brother, and I love you. I just don't want to see any of us suffer anymore. You have to really think about this, Hogan. You have to see that coming back home with us is for the best."

Hogan did try hard to follow his sister's speech. She sounded just like when they were kids, trying to keep him out of trouble. But he couldn't keep the dreams at bay. They commanded his thoughts, which eventually guided the words.

"I saw the preacher man in my dreams," he uttered.

They all looked at him, unsure of how to respond.

"The same preacher that was on the television before I got on the bus and came here."

Hogan tried his best to make them understand.

"That morning was cool, about 30 degrees, I think. I remember the sky. It was blue, like the curtains in Mommy's kitchen window. And the man that drove the bus was nice. He had on brown pants and shirt with a hat that matched too. I don't know why he thought my name was Buddy. But the preacher man said a man should find something called redemption if he wanted God to forgive him. I reckoned I couldn't find it there in Indiana, so I left."

Mommy's tears flowed, listening to Hogan explain his version of the past 27 years.

"People are mean everywhere... and people are nice too. I learned that. I reckon I wanted to go home to Kentucky so bad; I dreamed I was there the whole time I was sleeping. I must've been smiling a lot cause it made me feel real happy. Then the preacher showed up. He talked to me and said it wouldn't ever be like that anymore. You were all there too, at the church meeting. We sang and sang. But the preacher man talked louder. He told me that the redemption meant I had to forgive me for being dumb and not always knowing what to do. He said then God would forgive me, and you would too."

The room fell silent with the exception of occasional sniffles. Daddy put his hand on Mommy's shoulder as if to say their son would indeed be just fine.

"I'm home now, here, in Virginia. You don't have to worry about me no more. I won't be needing the drink no more either."

Hugs, tears, and a long-awaited peace drew out of the moment. As much as they all believed in the deep-seated superstitions of their people, they believed more that God's plan trumps all. Perhaps Hogan's troubled life was for this purpose.

God must have known he was stronger than anyone could imagine; stronger than the torment, stronger than the ones who thought they were smarter, strong enough to endure and recover when most would have given up altogether. Hogan understood that everyone must be accepted, even in their weakness; especially he must accept himself. In the moment of deepest despair, don't just sing down the preacher; stop, listen and remember the details.

They all stayed on long enough to complete necessary arrangements and help Hogan get his home in order.

Miss Marty was thrilled to know he would stay on. She readily agreed for him to help with gardening and other up-keep work around her house in exchange for rent. His Social Security check would more than take care of everything else.

This time though, he wouldn't separate himself from family. There would be many visits back and forth and joyful reunions for years to come.

*****

137

Early next fall, the Watts took a trip back to Lost Creek. Even in the depths of their secluded holler, progress found a way, by means of a widened dirt road and electrical power lines.

They followed the road down to the old swing bridge that separated their ridge from civilization. Barely passable, the wooden and rope bridge creaked and moaned under the weight of its passengers.

As if time had never passed, they traveled with ease to the Watts Cemetery. Bigger now, by the addition of new graves, the sight still held the same fascination. The original headstones remained in the middle, well preserved, as the nucleus of their family and their world.

Instinctively, they began the centuries-old task of clearing fallen limbs and other debris while reminiscing about old times. High above them, a bald eagle soared. Its cry caught their attention, causing them to look up as it circled the wooded edge where they stood.

Not a word was spoken. But they all felt it. The spirit of their family flew free on that eagle's wings. It made them think how a guardian angel had watched and is watching, over them, no matter where they call home. Once again, there was peace among them.

About the Author

Darlene Nixon is a Christian with professional experience in banking and journalism. Before tackling the position of Executive Director for Hart County Habitat for Humanity, Nixon served the local Habitat for Humanity affiliate since 2006 as both volunteer and board member.

Nixon has always shown a passion for writing, enjoying her God-given talent in several venues. She wrote as a news reporter for The News Leader newspaper in Royston, Georgia, as well as the Athens Daily News. Her novel, Singing Down the Preacher, was first published in 2011. Singing Down the Preacher details a fictional version of her Melungeon ancestry from Eastern Kentucky to Southern Indiana. The Condition of Living: Building, Binding, Healing the Habitat Way, was published in 2016. The novel honors the emotional impact of bringing people together through actively volunteering on a Habitat for Humanity house build.

Originally from a small farming community in Southern Indiana, Nixon now resides in NE Georgia with her husband, Hubert. The couple boasts two daughters and seven grandchildren.

 Connect with Darlene on Facebook:
https://www.facebook.com/darlene.nixon.161